The spinni[ng] finally stop[ped]

A mixture of curse[s] ~~and cries of~~ glee came from around the table.

Mack Bolan watched the man with the dark hair casually slip his hand inside the gray suit coat. The move was smooth, practiced.

The Executioner's battle radar went to red. Without conscious thought, his hand dropped to the butt of his Desert Eagle.

At the same time, he saw a clear plastic hypodermic needle appear in the man's fist. The big .44 was halfway out of the holster when Bolan felt someone slam into his side.

Holding the needle in an ice-pick grip, his thumb on the plunger, the dark-haired man raised it over his head.

As he brought his left arm up to block, the warrior felt a pair of hands grasp his elbow and wrist, halting the movement.

Helpless, Bolan could do nothing but watch the needle descend.

MACK BOLAN ®

The Executioner

DON PENDLETON'S
EXECUTIONER®
THE
TRIBURST

THE ARMS TRILOGY

★ BOOK II ★

A GOLD EAGLE BOOK FROM

WORLDWIDE®

TORONTO • NEW YORK • LONDON
AMSTERDAM • PARIS • SYDNEY • HAMBURG
STOCKHOLM • ATHENS • TOKYO • MILAN
MADRID • WARSAW • BUDAPEST • AUCKLAND

First edition April 1995
ISBN 0-373-61196-X

Special thanks and acknowledgment to
Jerry VanCook for his contribution to this work.

TRIBURST

Printed in U.S.A.

For Man's grim Justice goes its way,
And will not swerve aside:
It slays the weak, it slays the strong,
It has a deadly stride.

—*The Ballad of Reading Gaol, I*
Oscar Wilde

Every day of life the predators strive to bend or break the law. Yet no man is above the law and justice will be served.

—Mack Bolan

To the dedicated men and women of the ATF

1

The images on both sides of the split television screen could be summed up in one word—somber.

Mack Bolan's eyes blurred with fatigue as he stared at the TV. His left hand rose to his face, rubbing the clouds away beneath the lids. He opened his eyes once more and returned his gaze to the screen.

The man known as the Executioner focused on the left-hand side of the screen, the video camera's portrayal of the War Room located beneath the main house at Stony Man Farm. Seated around the conference table were Aaron Kurtzman, Barbara Price, Hal Brognola and the three members of Stony Man's stateside counterstrike force, Able Team.

The warrior's weary eyes moved to the other monitor. Yakov Katzenelenbogen and the rest of the commandos who made up Phoenix Force stared back at him.

Hal Brognola, the director of Sensitive Operations for Stony Man Farm, rose from his chair at the head of the table. "You got visual contact, Striker?" he asked, using Bolan's mission code name.

"I see you, Hal," the Executioner answered, "and I hear you."

"Katz?" Brognola asked.

"Loud and clear," Katzenelenbogen replied.

"Any problems getting the tele-satellite hookup?" Brognola wanted to know.

Bolan watched as Yakov Katzenelenbogen shook his head. "Negative. I went through an old Mossad friend. We are at a remote and abandoned outpost near the Syrian border." He paused. "My friend owed me a favor. His supervisors do not know that we are here."

A thin smile curled Brognola's lips as he nodded, and Bolan could practically read his old friend's mind. As far as the world at large knew—and that included allied agencies like the Mossad and even America's own CIA—Stony Man Farm, hidden deep within the Blue Ridge Mountains, didn't exist.

Stony Man Farm's overall objective was simple— move in where conventional law enforcement had failed and get the job done quickly and efficiently. Its chain of command was just as unadorned. Brognola, as director of Sensitive Operations, reported directly to, and took orders from, the President of the United States. Able Team, Phoenix Force and the other members of the Stony Man team answered only to the director.

Mack Bolan didn't answer to anyone—except his own conscience, and his strong sense of right and wrong. But the Executioner had maintained an arm's-length working relationship with Stony Man since leaving his position as the Farm's top operative, and still worked compatibly with the other teams during times of national emergency.

This was one of those times.

"Striker?" Brognola said, shifting his gaze on the screen. "Randall fix you up all right?"

Bolan turned and nodded into the video camera to the side of the screen. Brognola had gotten what they needed using Stony Man's typical clandestine method of dealing with other agencies: Brognola to the President, the President to the CIA director. And before you knew it, Dick Randall, the chief of station in Dublin, had orders to provide a big man going by the name Mike Belasko with a tele-satellite hookup.

"We're fixed up fine," Bolan answered. "No problems."

"Good. Then let's get down to business." He paused and cleared his throat, then glanced at the open manila file folder on the table in front of him. "What appeared at first to be three unrelated missions have overlapped. I no longer doubt a connection." He glanced up at the camera. "Anyone want to disagree?"

"No," both Bolan and Katz said.

Brognola turned to Carl Lyons at his side. The Able Team leader shook his head.

"Okay," the big Fed continued. "We originally thought we simply had an international assassin-for-hire calling himself the Huntsman. The only thing that smelled fishy was the conflicting physical descriptions, and those could have been explained by the use of disguise, the unreliability of the average witness, or a combination of both. But Striker's now taken out two people—one man, one woman—bent on assassinating the British prime minister. Both claimed to be the Huntsman. And for some reason, both were carrying bottle caps from Vietnamese beer bottles.'' He paused to let it sink in. ''There's another Huntsman in Israel, running with the Bloody Wind terrorists who're doing their damnedest to screw up the Israeli-Palestinian talks.'' Brognola pulled the stub of a partially chewed cigar from his breast pocket, started to stick it in his mouth, then set it on the table. ''All three of these assassins not only say they're the Huntsman, the seem to believe it. By the way, it turns out that the woman was an American security expert who worked for Weinacre Guards. She went missing in Europe four years ago and was presumed dead.''

''Defection?'' Katz asked.

Brognola shrugged. ''Maybe. We've got people looking into it, but so far there doesn't seem to be any connection.''

''I've got a feeling there will be,'' Bolan said. ''Somewhere there's a key, and we've got to find it, Hal.''

The Justice man nodded. ''Okay,'' he said. ''The second link is the weapons angle. The Russian freighter Able Team took on at Sitka was smuggling more than just the Russian small arms we'd expected.

There were M-16s and other American weapons on board. They've been traced back to the hijacking of several transport trucks that left a U.S. base in Europe."

"What about the Russian-made weapons we seized from Bloody Wind?" Katz said. "Have you identified them?"

Brognola turned to his other side, away from Lyons.

Aaron "The Bear" Kurtzman, Stony Man's computer genius, looked up from his wheelchair. "The serial numbers of the rifles Able Team got are consecutive to the ones you turned up over there," Kurtzman said. "You might not be able to prove it in a court of law, but I have no doubt they came from the same shipment."

"Yeah," Brognola said. "And my task force fell across more of them headed for a street gang in Atlanta, along with a shipment of the counterfeit money that's entered the picture. There's a connection, all right. And I haven't even gotten into the funny-money angle yet."

Bolan watched the big Fed close the file on the table, move it to the side, then open another manila folder.

"Basically the bad bills are good," Brognola stated. "Damn good. The best we've ever seen. They even pass through the Treasury's detection machines. The bills my task force has turned up match the ones Able Team found with the Russian weapons." The Justice man flipped a page within the folder and opened his mouth to speak again.

The sudden blast of automatic submachine-gun fire halted him.

Bolan's gaze shot to the other side of the screen in time to see the men of Phoenix Force dive for cover. As he watched, Calvin James and Gary Manning raised the Uzis slung over their shoulders and fired at a target off-screen. Former British SAS officer David McCarter responded with his Browning Hi-Power pistol.

Katz and Rafael Encizo had disappeared from the scope of the camera.

"Katz!" Brognola shouted from the other side of the television. "Katz! What—"

Bolan never heard the rest of the big Fed's speech. It was drowned out by another burst of automatic fire. But this volley didn't come from the screen in front of his eyes.

The new assault ripped through the thin wall separating him from the outer office of the CIA's Dublin headquarters, and sent the Executioner diving to the floor.

THE STEEL FINGERS of Bolan's right hand wrapped around the grips of the Desert Eagle. More submachine-gun rounds pocked the wall that divided him from the large bullpen just outside the door.

Bolan stayed under the fire, waiting. The door was locked, but sooner or later, one of the attackers would tire of shooting blindly through the wall and kick it in to check his handiwork.

The kick came sooner.

The door flew open, and the man who stepped across the threshold might as well have had IRA printed across his forehead. Bushy red hair sprouted from the sides of his leather cap. The wild eyes set within the ruddy face swept the office as a darker man followed his leader into the room, stopping directly behind the redhead.

The red-haired subgunner's eyes came to rest on the Executioner. A Heckler & Koch MP-5 swung over and down.

Bolan pulled the trigger, and a massive .44 Magnum round exploded from the barrel of the Desert Eagle. Traveling at almost 1200 feet per second, the jacketed hollowpoint ripped through the gray sweatshirt worn by the redhead and exited his back in a flurry of blood, tissue and fragments of spinal column.

The bloody storm blew into the face of the second gunner, momentarily blinding him and bringing a coarse scream to his horrified lips.

Another trigger squeeze from the Executioner silenced the scream.

The third man through the door wore a Harris tweed sport coat and black turtleneck shirt. Seeing what had happened, he backtracked out a split second ahead of Bolan's third thundering .44 bullet. The round missed his chest by a hair, crashing into the wooden doorframe and sending a storm of splinters back into the CIA bullpen area.

Suddenly the gunfire quieted.

Bolan took advantage of the brief recess to roll behind a desk. Coming up on one knee, he leaned around the corner, aiming the Desert Eagle toward the doorway. He could hear the labored breathing of men feeling the stress of the attack. One, two, three... at least four more of the terrorists waited, planning their next move.

The warrior kept his eyes trained on the front sight of the .44 as his brain recalled the design of the building. O'Harkin Imports, read the sign on the glass door leading to the reception area at the front of the structure, Bridget O'Harkin, Proprietor. Just behind the entryway was the showroom where Argentinean leather goods, Chinese silk, carpets from the Middle East and other products from around the world could be viewed.

The CIA front was a legitimate business, and even showed a profit at the end of each year. But a sliding door behind one of the carpets on the showroom's back wall led to the building's real purpose. The large bullpen and smaller offices of the CIA's Dublin headquarters were sandwiched between the showroom and a large storage area at the rear of the building. A narrow hallway, hidden against the outer wall, bypassed the area, connecting the storage and showrooms.

The voice that spoke from the bullpen had a thick brogue. "Come out. We wish only to talk to you. You will not be hurt."

The Executioner couldn't restrain the sardonic smile that touched his lips. Right. Glancing to the side of the room opposite the doorway, Bolan saw the hidden entry to the connecting hall. He had risen to his feet when the terrorist spoke again.

"I will give you no further warnings. Come out now, or you will die."

Silently, swiftly, Bolan crept away from the desk to the wall. Tapping quietly on the corner of a framed print hanging eye-level, he watched a short panel beneath the picture swing open.

A second later, he ducked into the opening and closed it behind him.

The Executioner rose to a standing position, peering into a peephole cut through the painting. He saw the man in the tweed sport coat peek cautiously into the back office.

The Executioner slid the Desert Eagle into his hip holster, tracing along the wall in the darkness. When he came to the other end of the hidden passage, his eye pressed against another peephole.

On the other side of the wall he saw the showroom. Vacant.

Quietly Bolan drew the sound-suppressed Beretta 93-R, then pushed the door open and stepped into the room. Keeping one eye on the door to the bullpen, the Executioner hurried toward the reception area.

The attractive young receptionist still sat behind her desk in the same position she'd been in when Bolan entered the building an hour earlier. But now, the blond hair that had glistened under the bright overhead track lights was missing. All that remained were a few strands of wet, reddish black blood that dripped from above her ears down her shoulders.

A righteous fury rose in Bolan's soul.

Two men stood in the bullpen by the time the Executioner had doubled back on them. A third leaned cautiously against the door frame, his wool overcoat pressed against the splintered wood that had taken the last .44 Magnum round. All three faced away from the Executioner, aiming MP-5s at the door to the inner office. The bodies of six CIA agents lay on the floor.

Bolan worked fast.

A double tap of suppressed 9 mm rounds entered the back of the neck of the closest man in the bullpen. Two more hollowpoints split the skull of the gunman next to him.

The man leaning against the doorway had half turned when the Executioner hammered another duo of 9 mm parabellum bullets into his cheekbones.

All three terrorists fell to the floor.

Bolan drew the Desert Eagle again, transferring the Beretta to his left hand. He paused. The man in the turtleneck had to be in the inner office. The warrior cleared his throat before calling out through the open door. "Come on out," he paraphrased the man. "I don't want to hurt you. Just want to talk."

The man in the turtleneck didn't buy it any more than the Executioner had.

With a bloodcurdling scream, the terrorist appeared in the entryway. The MP-5 jerked and danced in his hands as he wildly sprayed the room.

Bolan stood steady, lining up the Desert Eagle's front post sight between the dovetails at the rear of the slide.

The boom of the Magnum round was deafening in the narrow bullpen.

The Executioner stepped over the body and reentered the inner office. He glanced to the television screen, noting that the left side had gone black. To the right, he saw that the men of Able Team and the rest of the Stony Man crew had cleared the War Room. Only Hal Brognola stood in front of the camera.

The Executioner stepped in front of his own camera and stared directly into the lens. "You still with me, Hal?"

Brognola nodded.

"You catch all of the show?"

"Most of it, big guy. At least what the camera picked up. Is it over?"

Bolan hit the release on the Desert Eagle and dropped the partially spent magazine. The metal box hit the floor with a shrill metallic ring. As he started to answer, the Executioner heard soft footsteps patter quickly across the showroom. The bell on the front door tinkled lightly as the door opened and closed.

One of the gunners had to have hidden. Now, he was making his escape.

"No, it's not over, Hal," the Executioner replied. "In fact, it hasn't even started yet."

THE FORMER MOSSAD OUTPOST near the Gaza Strip had once been a remote gasoline station. Purchased by the Mossad shortly after the Six-Day War in 1967, operatives masquerading as mechanics and pump attendants kept it open for nearly a decade. From their strategic position, they kept a careful eye on vehicles entering and leaving the area.

The Mossad had always known it would only be a matter of time before word of the service station's true purpose leaked out. When it finally did, the site was abandoned.

From the tele-satellite setup at the rear of the service station, Katz heard the first vehicle pull up outside as he listened to Brognola summarize the mission to date. A frown cracked the tight dust-and-sand-covered skin of his face.

The Phoenix Force leader hadn't posted a guard. The fact that the station had once been a Mossad outpost and had been deserted for years was now common knowledge in Israel. It was highly unlikely that travelers would mistake the site for a working business. That, combined with the dilapidated appearance of the building and grounds, had made it seem the perfect place to "hide in plain sight." Besides, Katz had wanted all five members of his team to be in on the meeting.

But now, as his nostrils filled with the stench of upcoming trouble, Yakov Katzenelenbogen mentally kicked himself.

Turning to Rafael Encizo, the Israeli nodded toward the front of the building. "Check it out," he whispered.

Encizo hurried to the hall that led to the front of the station. Katz kept one ear cocked as he listened to Brognola talk about the counterfeiting aspects of the mission.

Brognola was flipping through his file again when the first shots sounded.

Encizo came diving back through the doorway. "Bloody Wind!" the Cuban expatriate shouted as he swung his Uzi back toward the hallway. "Two vans. Maybe a dozen men."

The warriors of Phoenix Force had fought the bloody battle for democracy together too long to need orders. As Katz racked the bolt of his 9 mm mini-Uzi submachine pistol with his prosthetic hand, he saw James, McCarter and Manning dive to the floor and roll to defensive positions around the room.

"Katz!" Hal Brognola's voice shouted over the airwaves. "Katz! What—"

The first man through the door kept the Phoenix Force leader from answering. Wielding a semiauto Franchi LAW-12, the terrorist fired a blast of double-aught buck. The expanding, flesh-ripping pattern sailed past Katz's shoulders, the BB-like pellets missing him by inches.

Katz held down the mini-Uzi's trigger, blasting a full-auto burst of 9 mm hollowpoints into the khaki field jacket above the shotgun. The terrorist's mouth opened in shock as the rounds shredded both of his lungs. He sucked a deep breath, then blood shot from his mouth as he exhaled and tumbled to the floor.

Two more khaki-clad men burst into the room. The first gunner rattled off a full-auto burst from a Walther MPL. The bullets raced past James at the rear window, shattering the glass.

James and McCarter teamed up on the man, both cutting loose with short volleys that dropped the terrorist to the oil-stained tile.

The surviving gunner's gaze locked on his fallen comrades as he entered the room. He froze momentarily, the German MP-40 in his hands lowering. Then his muscles jerked in fear, sending a burst of autofire into the floor.

His hesitation cost him his life.

Rafael Encizo, firing from the prone position, unleashed a torrent of 9 mm parabellum rounds into the man's belly, chest and face.

Katz sprinted to the rear window and spotted one lone gunman rounding the corner of the building.

The mini-Uzi dropped the man in his tracks.

"Rafe! Gary! David!" the Phoenix Force leader shouted above the ongoing gunfire. "Stay here! Cal, with me!"

Katz took another look through the window, then vaulted the sill, dropping to a squatting position as another gunner rounded the corner. The man's feet hit the fallen body of the terrorist Katz had downed a moment earlier and tripped, sprawling into the dust.

Katz fired as the man fell, letting the mini-Uzi follow the somersault. By the time the terrorist rolled to a halt, he was dead.

The Phoenix Force leader moved to the left of the window. He dropped the nearly empty 25-round magazine from his weapon and rammed another home as Calvin James came hurtling through the window. The former Navy SEAL moved automatically to the right.

Pressing their backs against the sun-warmed concrete of the building, the two warriors covered both corners.

"Circle toward the front," Katz said as the gun battle continued to rage inside the service station. "We've got to close them in."

James nodded, then turned and moved cautiously toward his corner.

Katz did the same in the other direction. He heard a quick burst of gunfire to his rear and glanced over his shoulder in time to see another Bloody Wind gunman fall to Calvin James's bullets.

James didn't bother turning to face Katz. He simply raised his left hand over his shoulder, his thumb and index finger circling into the "okay" sign, then moved on.

Katz dropped to one knee, then inched an eye around the concrete to the side of the building. He saw a man moving warily along the wall. Three days' growth of beard spotted the gunner's face, and in his hands, Katz saw the bullpup stock of an Austrian-made AUG battle rifle.

The Phoenix Force leader moved back a step and waited.

A few seconds later, he heard the quiet footsteps stop just around the corner. Changing grips on the mini-Uzi, he hooked his thumb over the trigger and extended it around the wall.

Katz heard a puny shriek as he thumbed the trigger, firing blindly around the corner. He changed grips again and darted out into the open.

The random rounds had gut-shot the approaching terrorist. The man lay bleeding on the ground in agony.

Another quick tap of the mini-Uzi's trigger ended his suffering.

Katz reloaded again, jamming the half-empty clip into one of the canvas carrier pouches at his waist. He moved swiftly now, his gaze glued to the front of the building. Making the corner without further incident, he dropped once more to one knee.

Two Bloody Wind gunners stood back-to-back as they guarded the building. A clean-shaved man faced the doorway, while his mustachioed comrade stared straight ahead, looking back at the parked vans Encizo had mentioned.

Katz leaned around the corner and squeezed the trigger.

A full-auto burst of fire stitched from the clean-shaved man's waist, up his ribs and into his neck. He fell forward into the doorway of the service station.

The mustachioed man didn't even look toward the source of the assault. He merely dropped his rifle and sprinted toward the van.

Katz turned the mini-Uzi toward him, squeezed the trigger and heard only a gritty, crunching click.

The Phoenix Force leader ducked back around the corner, his eyes dropping to the bolt of his weapon. Oily sand and dirt clung to its frame.

Drawing the bolt back manually, Katz felt it lock up. He cursed quietly as he let the weapon fall from his hands and drew the Beretta 92 from his belt holster.

The Uzi had been designed to withstand the filth of battle in regions such as this. But nothing was infallible, and this weapon had been fired unmercifully over the past few days with no opportunity for cleaning. Combine that with the sand and dirt that filled the air constantly, and it was a miracle the weapon hadn't jammed earlier.

The gunfire inside the building continued as Katz looked back around the corner. The cowardly terrorist with the mustache had disappeared in the vicinity of the vans.

A sudden figure appeared in the Phoenix Force leader's peripheral vision. He swung the Beretta that way, his finger lightening on the trigger as he saw James round the opposite corner.

The American warrior nodded that things were clear on his side.

Katz motioned toward the vans. The closer, a blue Chevy, was parked on the other side of the concrete foundation where the gas pumps had once stood. The second, an older model Ford, stood behind it to one side.

The Phoenix Force warriors started discreetly toward the vehicles from both angles. The man with the mustache had had no time to hide anywhere else. He had to have taken refuge in, or behind, one of the vans.

Halfway there, Katz heard the Chevy's engine roll over. Looking in through the open window, he saw the top of the mustachioed man's head leaning low over the steering wheel.

The Phoenix Force leader fired two rounds into the vehicle's front tire, then swept his weapon back toward the rear. Another double tap took out the rear tire and the van dropped, angling toward him on the wheel rims.

James had sprinted to the other side of the vehicle as soon as Katz opened up. The Phoenix Force leader heard a burst of 9 mm rounds. The van straightened itself as James blew the other two tires.

Inside the vehicle, the terrorist threw up his hands. Katz could see him screaming, but the gunfire from inside the station drowned out his words.

Then, suddenly, the gunfire halted.

"Please! Please! I surrender!" screamed the voice inside the Chevy.

Katz moved out in front of the vehicle where he could still watch the station as he approached the driver's door. The fight inside had ended.

"Move and I'll kill you," Katz told the man in the van. Then, keeping one eye on his prisoner, he turned his Beretta toward the front of the building.

A moment later Manning's voice came through the doorway. "All clear?" the big Canadian asked.

"Almost," Katz said. The Beretta trained through the open window once more, he pried the van's door open with his prosthetic limb.

"Get out," he ordered.

The terrorist remained frozen, his hands locked around the steering wheel.

James appeared beside the vehicle and manhandled the terrorist from the vehicle. The recreant continued to whimper as he tumbled to the dirt and gravel at Katz's feet. "Please do not kill me!" he pleaded.

Katz rested the muzzle of the Beretta on the bridge of the man's nose. The terrorist closed his eyes, believing that his fate had been sealed. But the Phoenix Force leader knew that the man might be able to provide valuable information into exactly what was going on. He needed to be interrogated, but not here. By now a passing motorist would have reported the gunfire, and troops would soon arrive to check it out.

Katz left the Beretta's barrel resting on the terrorist's nose as he leaned down and whispered into the man's ear. "I won't shoot you. At least not now." He paused, cocking the double-action hammer for emphasis. "But if you don't answer the questions we ask you, by the time I'm through doing what I *will* do, you will be begging for a bullet."

2

A variety of quickly changing emotions rolled through Aaron Kurtzman's soul as he watched the gun battles unfold on screen in Stony Man Farm's War Room. First came shock as the computer wizard realized that the two "safe" locations that had been chosen to set up the satellite links hadn't been safe at all.

The next emotion that flooded Kurtzman's soul was known to most men simply as fear. Some analyzed the sensation further, recognizing it as actually being the "flight or fight" instinct that had enabled mankind and other species to survive centuries of evolution.

Only a very select few—Kurtzman and the other men and women of Stony Man Farm being among the elite group—had delved even deeper than that into the emotion of fear. They realized the feeling could be molded, worked with, and used as a source of energy in battle.

As Kurtman stared at the split screen, the left side suddenly went black. As Bolan fought on to the right, the men of Phoenix Force disappeared into the darkness as if sucked into the bowels of hell.

"There's nothing we can do," Hal Brognola said. "They're on their own."

Kurtzman was already wheeling back from the conference table when he answered, "For now, maybe. But when its over, they'll need help. And I'm damned if I intend to sit here watching television when I've got work to do." His callused palms rolled the wheels toward the elevator door in the corner of the War Room.

Behind him, Kurtzman heard the rest of the assembled Stony Man team rise in their seats and force themselves away from the screen toward their various assignments. The mission would have to go on.

Kurtzman ascended to the Computer Room. Carmen Delahunt, Huntington Wethers, and Akira Tokaido were hard at work in front of their keyboards as he wheeled past them and up the ramp to his own bank of computer screens.

The Stony Man computer wizard ran a hand through his hair, then settled down to the task at hand. Within minutes he had linked into the CIA's intelligence files, bypassing the codes and traps set up to keep him and other "hackers" out. With a frown of concentration he went about the task of searching the files for all info pertaining to the Huntsman.

There was more than one Huntsman. What linked them together? Common training? They all operated with similar MOs thus far. The Vietnamese beer bottle caps—whatever the hell those were for. Common political belief? Kurtzman hesitated. Maybe. So far that wasn't definite.

Running his hand through his hair once more, Kurtzman sat back in his wheelchair. The big question was, how did they keep turning up in so many diverse terrorist groups around the world? The computer man stared at the screen. Was the link between the various terrorist groups even stronger than was suspected? Or was some other junction overlooked?

He felt a hand on his shoulder. In the reflection of the screen in front of him, he saw the trim outline of Barbara Price.

"Striker's okay," the Stony Man mission controller said. "Hal just talked to him."

Kurtzman breathed a sigh of relief. Mack Bolan was the best warrior he'd ever known; maybe the best there'd ever been. But even the best had a bullet waiting for him somewhere, and Aaron Kurtzman was comforted by the knowledge that wherever Bolan's bullet was, it hadn't been in one of the guns of the men who had just attacked.

"What about Phoenix Force?" he asked Price as he exited the CIA connection.

The woman shrugged. "Camera still isn't working." She squeezed Kurtzman's shoulder reassuringly, then her image disappeared from the screen.

Kurtzman began the tedious process of entering the files of Israel's Mossad. When he was finished with the Israelis, there would be Britain's MI-6, then the French, Germans, Russian, Japanese...

He knew he had a long day—probably several long days—in front of him. But somewhere there was a link, an answer to the what and why of the intricate scheme of which he suspected the Huntsman was only part. Kurtzman was determined to find it. The lives of Mack Bolan, the men of Able Team and Phoenix Force, not to mention legions of innocent bystanders, might well depend upon his ability to quickly unravel the mystery.

Kurtzman sighed again and continued to tap the keyboard. Innocent human lives at stake?

Nothing new for Stony Man Farm.

Outside Cody, Wyoming

FROM HIS SEAT next to Stony Man pilot Charlie Mott, Carl Lyons watched the ragged formations of the Big Horn Mountains fly by beneath the Beechcraft Baron. The former LAPD detective's mind drifted a hundred years into the past, to the era of the United States's Indian Wars.

The Custer Battlefield, a few miles farther north in Montana, had hosted the most famous battle of that time period. But the Big Horn region had seen countless other engagements pitting the U.S. Cavalry against the Sioux, the other tribes of the area, and often coalitions of the tribes. Little Big Horn, where the united Sioux, Cheyenne and Arapaho peoples destroyed General George Armstrong Custer and his men, was the best example of those coalitions.

Lyons continued to watch the scenic view below. The Big Horn Mountains, and the Rockies they were quickly approaching, had been the home of many bloody battles.

The Beechcraft's wheels hit the runway, and Lyons saw the two vehicles at the end of the short landing strip. As Mott taxied slowly forward, the tiny figures on each side of the Chevy sedan grew larger.

The two Justice Department agents could have been bookends. Both wore white shirts, subtle paisley ties and blue suits. The tails of their jackets danced in the hard Wyoming wind, and their ties had blown over their shoulders. But both men's light brown hair had been so heavily sprayed that rather than wave, it simply shifted back and forth in time to the rising and falling gusts.

"Frick and Frack?" Charlie Mott asked no one in particular as he came to a halt. "Or is it Tweedledee and Tweedledum?" He turned toward Lyons, grinning.

"What brand of hair spray you suppose they use?" Hermann "Gadgets" Schwarz asked from his seat behind Lyons. "Helmet in a Can?"

"Okay, okay," Lyons said, opening the door next to him. "We've got work to do." He dropped to the ground and walked around the side of the plane to where the two men stood waiting.

"Special Agents Mullins and Mallett," the man on the right said, flipping open a credential case. A key ring hung from his fingers on the other side of the blue suit. "I'm Mullins. You're the three men Brognola called about?"

Lyons nodded. Up close now, the resemblance between the two men was even more remarkable than he'd imagined.

Schwarz and Rosario "Politician" Blancanales climbed from the plane and joined him. "You guys related or something?" Gadgets asked.

Both men frowned at Schwarz, puzzled. "No," both said.

Mullins turned back to Lyons. "Exactly who are you?"

Lyons looked the man in the eye. "What did Brognola tell you to do?" he asked.

Mullins glanced over his shoulder to the black Ford Blazer S10 Tahoe next to the Chevy. "Provide unmarked transport with room for various equipment."

"Did he tell you to ask questions?" Lyons queried, holding the stare.

"Well . . . no."

"Then give me the keys," Lyons said.

The Able Team leader took the key ring as Schwarz, Blancanales and Mott began to unload the equipment from the Beechcraft. "Thanks," he said simply, then moved behind the Blazer's wheel.

A few minutes later, the vehicle was heading down a blacktop road into Cody, Wyoming.

"What's this guy's name again?" Gadgets asked as he began to instal the programmable police radio and punch in the codes for Stony Man Farm and the local police frequencies.

"Watson," Lyons said, recalling the file he'd raced through on Kurtzman's computer screen. "Gilbert Watson. They call him 'Van Gogh.'"

"Van Gogh?" Blancanales asked, looking up from the back seat where he was loading the 50-round helical drum magazine of a Calico M-961 A concealable submachine gun. "A one-eared counterfeiter, or what?"

"He's an artist," Lyons replied as they topped a short rise and the outskirts of Cody appeared. "One of the top funny-bucks men in the world. He got tagged with Van Gogh because he's schizophrenic. One violent SOB himself, and he always employs several hardcases to cover his back." He guided the Blazer onto a four-lane highway and slowed as they reached the city limits. Ahead, he saw the statue of a goateed man holding a lever-action carbine astride a horse.

A few moments later, the Able Team leader followed a curve past the statue in front of the Buffalo Bill Historical Center, then jogged to the right and headed for downtown Cody.

"We got an address for ol' Van?" Schwarz asked as he finished with the radio.

Lyons shook his head. "Negative. But Intel says he's grown fond of the cooking at the Irma Hotel. Eats lunch there three, sometimes four times a week."

They entered the downtown area, cruising slowly past a variety of Western stores and souvenir shops. The town was alive with tourists who all seemed to be sporting walking shoes, shorts and cheap, felt cowboy hats. Each business, either on the sign above it or the front window, displayed some sort of likeness of William F. Cody, the famed scout and Wild West show performer who had settled the area.

The Irma Hotel appeared on the right, a stone and wood construction typical of the period in which it was built. A brown-and-white picket rail ran around the porch on the second story. A matching sign hung over the front entrance. Schwarz read it out loud. "The Irma, Buffalo Bill's Original Hotel in the Rockies."

Lyons saw a parking space and pulled in parallel to a store selling beaded shirts and handmade buckskins. The men of Able Team exited the Blazer and started toward the hotel.

They crossed the street, entered the Irma's front door and followed a sign to the crowded restaurant. A waitress wearing a Western hat, skirt and blouse led them to an empty booth against the wall, beneath a row of framed yellow newspaper clippings that pertained to the exploits of Buffalo Bill Cody.

Lyons slid in across from Schwarz and Blancanales, sitting sideways so he could watch both entrances. Across the room, he saw the ornately carved wooden bar for which the Irma was famous.

The men of Able Team glanced at the menus, ordered "Buffalo" burgers and settled in as the waitress brought them each a tall bottle of Black Dog ale. The food had arrived when the man in a pale blue sport coat entered through the door to the hotel's registration area.

Lyons knew Gilbert Watson immediately, even though the man had grown a wild white handlebar mustache since the Stony Man photo had been taken. In a wide-brimmed straw hat and white western shirt, the portly counterfeiter waited patiently until the same waitress who'd seated Able Team found him a table in the corner.

The Able Team warriors had finished lunch by the time the waitress brought Watson a steaming bowl of soup with what was undoubtedly another Buffalo burger. Lyons picked up the check and looked up at Schwarz. "You got your walkie-talkie?"

Gadgets tapped his collar, indicating the remote mike hidden beneath his shirt.

Lyons nodded. "Wait outside in case he's on foot. Pol and I'll go get the car."

The three men rose. Lyons dropped a tip on the table, paid the bill and followed Blancanales out onto the sidewalk. He watched Schwarz cross the street to the window of a Western tack shop as he and Pol started back to the Blazer.

Fifteen minutes later, the radio scanner stopped on the private Stony Man frequency. "Able Two to One and Three," Gadgets's voice whispered.

Lyons lifted the mike. "Go."

"The mark just left the hotel. Coming your way. Sit tight."

Lyons looked up into the rearview mirror. A moment later, he saw the rotund counterfeiter cross the side street to the block where they were parked. As he watched, Watson fished a key ring out of his slacks, then walked to the driver's side of a late-model Nissan truck parked two spaces behind the Blazer.

Schwarz appeared behind him, a block back. "Want to take him on the street?" he asked over the airwaves.

Lyons considered it briefly. Then, thumbing the mike, he said, "No, it might attract attention. We'll follow him and take down the whole operation at once."

Watson pulled the Nissan onto the street and started forward. Lyons looked up at Schwarz, still a half block away. If Able Team's electronics man hurried, Watson might spot him. But if he didn't, the counterfeiter would have time to slip away in the heavy traffic.

Lifting the mike to his lips again, Lyons said, "Gadgets, just stay put. We'll follow him, find out where he goes, then swing back for you."

"Roger," Schwarz answered.

Lyons followed the Nissan down the street several blocks, leaving the "old town" tourist area and entering a more modern business section. The main thoroughfare curved south, passing the usual fast-food enterprises, shopping centers and car dealerships. Finally Watson turned off in front of a school.

The Able Team leader dropped back, giving the Nissan more room in the thinner traffic. They followed the counterfeiter into a residential area.

Lyons saw Pol watching the car ahead through a set of binoculars. "He look like he's spotted us?"

Blancanales shook his head. "Nope. He's not paying attention at all. Looks like he's even singing along with the radio."

The Nissan turned onto another side street, and Lyons hit the accelerator. As he turned the corner, Watson pulled into the driveway of a one-story brick house. The garage door began to rise.

The Able Team leader slowed again, creeping along and timing his pass after the Nissan had entered the garage. He looked into the shadowy area as they went by.

The Nissan was the only vehicle in the double garage as a dark figure opened the door to the outside, and Gilbert "Van Gogh" Watson struggled to squeeze his bulk through the opening. In the darkness, Lyons couldn't tell much about the man who helped him— just that he was taller than the chubby counterfeiter.

But what he saw told the Able Team leader all he needed to know.

Slung over the shoulder of Watson's lackey was the easily recognized outline of an Uzi submachine gun.

Dublin, Ireland

THE BELL ABOVE THE DOOR chimed as the Executioner holstered the Desert Eagle, threw the door of the import store open and stepped onto the streets of Dublin. The late-afternoon sidewalk was crowded with men and women hurrying home from work.

Bolan's trained eye darted up and down the street, finally falling on the back of a man with a long gray raincoat tossed carelessly over his shoulders. The man adjusted the coat as the Executioner watched, then adjusted it again.

He looked suspiciously like a man who was concealing something under a hurriedly donned garment.

The warrior looked down at the legs beneath the coattail. The man wore khaki fatigue pants tucked into black combat boots.

The bell chimed again as the door behind the Executioner closed. He started toward the man, letting a dozen people fall in between him and his prey, who glanced back twice over his shoulder, relieving the Executioner of any doubts that he might have picked the wrong guy.

Bolan drifted back farther as they neared a corner. There had been no opportunity to take any of the IRA terrorists at the CIA headquarters alive, and he needed this man breathing.

More importantly, he needed him talking.

At the first corner, the Executioner stepped up to a store window while the terrorist waited for the red light to turn green, then followed the man across the street in the crosswalk. A block later they turned left on Belgrade Square.

The Executioner watched the man finally slip his arms into the sleeves of his coat, still careful not to expose whatever was hidden under the long tail.

The man slowed as they reached a pub area, glanced over his shoulder again, then turned in under a sign that read Culturalann na hEireann. Bolan waited for the door to close, then hurried forward.

Irish folk music blared as the Executioner grasped the door handle and stepped into the dark pub. He moved quickly into the shadows, his eyes falling on the back of the gray overcoat as the man walked up to the bar on his right. The terrorist took a seat on one of the tall bar stools, then turned to watch the door.

The warrior kept one eye on the bar as he made his way around the room toward the back of the gray coat.

A red-faced Irishman bumped into the Executioner, the beer in his mug sloshing over the side onto Bolan's sport coat. "Son of a bitch, matey," the drinker bellowed. "I've wet yer fair cloak. So I stand you a free one, eh?"

Bolan hesitated. If he refused a drink when it was offered so forcefully, it might well cause a quarrel—attention the Executioner didn't need at the moment.

One the other hand, he hardly had time to sit down and get drunk with this man and his friends.

Bolan smiled, tapped his chest, then shook his head. "The old ticker," he said. "The doctor's forbidden me."

The drunk's smile faded, and his face became a mask of concern. "Ah, it happened with me father," he shouted above the music. "Personally I'd rather dance with the Prince of Darkness than lose me rights to the Holy Water." He draped an arm around the Executioner's shoulders and nodded toward a table. "Soda water it is, then. Come on, I'll introduce me mates."

The Executioner glanced up at the bar where the bartender was pouring a short glass of Southern Comfort for the man in the gray overcoat. Turning back to the drunk, he said, "Sorry, I've an appointment to keep."

The man laughed. "There's always time for a drink," he brayed, tightening his grip on Bolan's shoulders and turning the Executioner toward a table where four equally intoxicated men in leather jackets and caps sat downing whiskey and beer. "Be a sport, now."

Bolan made a quick 360-degree sweep of the bar to make sure no one was watching, then drove an elbow hard into the drunk's sternum. He heard a rush of air escape the man's lips. The man's eyes rolled back in his head and his knees buckled as he sank to the floor.

The warrior stepped quickly away, his eyes moving to the man's table. He saw one of the men in the leather jackets throw back his head and laugh, then slap the shoulder of the man next to him. "Have a look, Neil. Old Frank's had one too many and dropped to the floor!"

Bolan moved on, gradually making his way behind the man at the bar as he circled the room. He hadn't enjoyed doing what he had just been forced to do, but it had become obvious that the drunk didn't plan to take no for an answer.

When he had reached a vantage point behind the terrorist, the warrior moved swiftly up to the bar behind him. Drawing the Desert Eagle, he leaned into the counter and held it in front of him but out of sight.

The bartender walked forward.

"Guinness," Bolan said.

The man in the gray coat turned toward him. In his early fifties, his brown eyebrows were a shade lighter than his hair. His nose told the Executioner he had fought his share of rounds, either in, or out of, the ring.

Bolan saw the uncertain stare in his eyes. Then, the eyes widened as the terrorist recognized the warrior from the CIA headquarters battle.

Beneath the bar, Bolan shoved the barrel of the big .44 into the man's ribs. "Just keep quiet," he whispered through his clenched teeth. He glanced down at the man's coat. Somewhere beneath the gray wool was the weapon, or weapons, the terrorist had tried to conceal during his walk from the CIA offices. He needed to disarm the man at the earliest opportunity, but there was no way to do so in the crowded bar without someone seeing the procedure.

The bartender set a glass of thick-foamed stout on the bar as the band broke into a rousing rendition of "Lilly the Pink." Bolan reached into his pocket with his free hand and dropped a pound note beside it. Looking back to the man on the other end of the Desert Eagle, he said, "Finish your drink. Then we go. You do as you're told, and there's a chance you might get out of all this alive."

The man's face broke into an inappropriate smile. He threw the shot of Southern Comfort back in one motion, then drained the remainder of his ale and stood.

Bolan tucked the Desert Eagle under his jacket and rose next to him. "Walk straight for the door," he ordered, "and don't forget what's under my coat."

The man in the gray coat chuckled, then said, "I *will* get out of this alive." He turned and started toward the door. "Do you know why?" he shouted over his shoulder above the music.

Bolan didn't answer. He prodded the man forward with his free hand, hoping that what he suspected was about to happen, wouldn't.

"Because the Huntsman cannot die!" the man roared at the top of his lungs as his hand disappeared under the coat.

Bolan lunged forward.

He was a microsecond slow.

The terrorist shoved the barrel of a small black automatic pistol into his mouth. A moment later, the back of his head exploded, throwing a volcano of blood and brains into the air.

The man fell face-forward onto the wooden floor of the pub as the gun clattered down next to him.

Israel

THE BRIGHT BLUE WAVES of the Mediterranean Sea broke over the ragged stones of the coast as Yakov Katzenelenbogen watched through the sliding glass door. The only sound in the room was the soft purr of the microwave oven in the kitchen area to his side.

A momentary melancholy entered his soul. Israel had been his home by choice, rather than birth, and he felt the same love for this ancient land of his people that he suspected the parent of an adopted child felt toward his heir.

Behind him, in the living room, the former Mossad operative heard a metallic snap. Although he couldn't see the source of the noise, he knew what it had to be, and continued to stare at the water.

Katz's eyes lowered to the cedar porch outside the glass as the clicking sounded again. The safehouse had been provided by Ranon Goldberg, the same old Mossad friend who had set up the satellite connection from the outpost. A tiny grin played at the corners of Katz's lips. Ranon had directed Phoenix Force to the

Mossad hideout, made sure it was stocked with provisions and made sure it wouldn't be in use. Then he'd bowed politely out of the picture, saying he was needed in Tel Aviv. Apparently the man had other fish to fry.

Katz heard the click again and turned away from the glass, his eyes taking in the scene behind him. The living room of the seaside cottage had been decorated in Western decor, with knotty pine walls and a short indoor-outdoor carpet to resist the salt sea. McCarter, Manning and Encizo stood scattered around the room, their backs resting on the pale bronze wood.

To the Phoenix Force leader's right lay the small kitchen, the source of the humming microwave. Against the wall to his left stood a dark green captain's table and five chairs. The sixth wooden armchair of the dinette set had been pulled to the center of the room.

In it, tied and blindfolded, sat the mustachioed terrorist they had taken prisoner at the outpost. He had turned out to be a tougher nut to crack than Katz had first suspected, refusing to tell them anything except his first name: Jabbar.

That wasn't enough. Key information from him was vital. Katz knew the attack had been the work of Bloody Wind, a violent faction of Palestinian terrorists that had done its best to disrupt the new Israeli-Palestinian land talks the week before, as had Anvil of God.

The menacing click sounded again.

Katz turned toward Calvin James. The Phoenix Force warrior circled the chair, rhythmically flipping out the wickedly curved, serrated blade of a Spyderco Civilian folding knife. Each click jerked the blindfolded prisoner's head in the direction of the sound. Finally, as Katz watched, Jabbar broke.

"What in the name of God is it?" the terrorist screamed in Arabic. "What is that satanic noise?"

"We're so glad you asked," Katz said. The room returned to silence as James continued to circle, flipping the knife open, then closing it again without further explanation.

Katz studied the prisoner. He had concluded that the fear Jabbar expressed so openly was intentionally exaggerated—not an uncommon stalling technique. So now James was about to cut through the false fear, and instill the real thing in the man's heart. And no one Katz knew could do that better than Calvin Thomas James, formerly of the U.S. Navy SEALs.

James looked at Katz, who nodded.

The Stony Man warrior stood in front of Jabbar, holding the closed knife in an ice-pick grip. His ring finger entered the large round opening hole in the blade as his other hand moved to the blindfold. With lightning speed, James jerked the blindfold up off Jabbar's eyes, leaving it around the terrorist's forehead like a headband. At the same time he flipped the blade downward, the hooked point coming to a halt a quarter of an inch from the Arab's nose.

Sunlight streaked in through the glass door, reflecting off the blade and making Jabbar squint. He sucked in a lungful of air, but appeared too frightened to let it out.

James leaned low, his face an inch from the terrorist's.

Katz moved to one side of the room, taking up a vantage point where he could see both interrogator and subject. James smiled. "Do you speak English?" he asked.

Jabbar didn't answer. He continued to stare at the piece of ragged steel in front of his eyes.

The smile faded from James's face and was replaced by a scowl. "Do you speak English!" he thundered at the top of his voice.

"Yes! Yes!"

James straightened and nodded to Rafael Encizo. The Cuban disappeared into the kitchen.

He turned back to the man in the chair. Suddenly the hand holding the knife shot out. The curved needle tip hooked up under the blindfold still around the top of Jabbar's head. James pulled back and up.

A soft ripping sound broke the silence, then the blindfold divided in front and slid down Jabbar's neck to fall on his shoulders.

Encizo returned to the living room holding a large white cardboard box. The outside portrayed pictures of apples, potatoes and other fruits and vegetables beneath a company logo.

"Are you familiar with this knife?" James asked the man.

Jabbar nodded. "A *sabbit*," he whispered.

James chuckled. "Close, but no cigar. The design probably did come from that Indonesian blade, and it can be used similarly. But believe me, friend, this is even better. The blade works on two planes at the same time—both vertical and horizontal. But rather than just tell you, let me demonstrate." He turned toward Encizo.

The Cuban reached into the box and pulled out four raw carrots. He held them between his fingers, made a fist, then raised his arm.

James stepped forward, bringing the knife in close to his body. The curved blade slashed out, then back. A soft crunching sound echoed through the safehouse, then the tips of all four carrots toppled to the floor at Encizo's feet.

"First knuckle," James said. He repeated the process, the carrots shortened farther, and said, "Second knuckle." After the third sweep of the curved blade, carrots were barely visible above the back of Encizo's hand.

"Stub," James said. He turned back to Jabbar. "We'll leave your thumb for last. This thing's one hell of a slasher, huh?"

The Arab didn't answer. He stared wide-eyed ahead, his lower jaw falling open.

Encizo reached into the box again and produced a cluster of deep purple grapes. Picking two, he dropped the rest back in the box, then set it on the floor at his feet. He turned, smiled at Jabbar, then held a grape in front of each of his eyes.

"You got woodpeckers back home in Iraq?" James asked Jabbar.

"Wood...*what?*" the terrified man asked.

Katz translated the question into Arabic. Jabbar nodded, puzzled.

"This thing works kind of like a woodpecker, sometimes," James said. He turned toward Encizo in flurry of motion.

The Civilian leaped out, sinking into the first grape, then the second. As the hooked blade returned to James's side, clear sticky fluid burst from the punctured skin.

The microwave bell pinged. James nodded to Gary Manning, and the big Canadian disappeared into the kitchen.

Interrogations like this one were all a matter of timing. James was a master at that timing. Questioning wouldn't begin until he saw in Jabbar's face that the moment was exactly right.

Manning returned to the living room carrying a huge turkey leg.

"Hold it up," James said. He turned toward Jabbar. "This knife is an excellent extractor, as well. Watch."

With the opening hole and hooked tip, the blade looked like the beak of some predatory bird as James held it in front of him. But it performed more like the claw of that bird as it sank down into the turkey flesh, twisted, then came up with the snapping segments of several white tendons.

Jabbar gasped.

James turned back to the man. "Thus ends the lesson. Oh, there's other tricks I could show you, like have one of these men hold a banana about crotch level while I rend it to shreds." Gradually his tone began to harden. "But if you haven't caught on yet, Jabbar, you're not going to." Slowly he started across the room toward the horrified man.

Jabbar's gaze was glued to the blade. "What... what are you going to—"

James crossed the rest of the room with one great leap. "Oh, you want it straight? Don't like symbolism, huh? Okay, first I'm gonna slice your fingers down to stubs! Then I'm gonna extract the tendons from your arms and legs so that you'll never walk or use those arms again." The blade slashed through the air several times in front of the wild-eyed terrorist. "If that doesn't work, say goodbye to your eyes, and if all else fails..." He let his voice trail off, then turned to Encizo.

The Cuban fished through the cardboard box, came up with a yellow banana and tossed it toward James.

James's arm flashed through the air twice, and the banana fell to the floor in three pieces. He turned back to Jabbar and hooked the knife gently under the man's chin, pulling up to force the Arab to meet his eyes.

A lone drop of blood seeped from the terrorist's chin and ran down his throat as the tip of the blade bit into the skin.

"If all else fails, Jabbar," James said softly, "it'll be banana time."

The man in the chair turned his head to the side and emptied the contents of his stomach onto the carpet.

James waited until the retching had turned to dry heaves. "Now," he said, "would you like to start talking and avoid all that?"

Jabbar nodded his agreement.

James stepped to the side as David McCarter took his place. The former British SAS officer produced a clean white piece of paper and an ink pad. "First thing we do, mate, is get a few prints, eh?"

James closed the knife and clipped it to the back of his pants as he crossed the room to Katz. The Phoenix Force leader motioned him back toward the sliding glass door.

"Well done, as usual," Katz said, when they were out of earshot. He glanced toward the kitchen. "Should we grab a bite while we wait for David?"

James chuckled. "As long as it's not fruit, vegetables or turkey," he whispered. "Damn, Katz, sometimes I make *myself* sick. Can you imagine really doing that kind of stuff to anyone?"

The Israeli shook his head. "No. But there are people who do." He nodded toward Jabbar. "Probably him, or at least some of his friends."

"Don't know what I'm gonna do if anybody ever calls my bluff," he said, then turned toward the kitchen. "Yeah, come on, I guess. Let's eat."

3

Three old men sat whittling sticks on a bench in front of the Irma Hotel as Lyons pulled the Blazer up to the curb.

Schwarz, sitting on the end of the bench, leaned against one of the white-and-brown posts that supported the second-floor porch. A cheap, gray felt cowboy hat rested at a cocky angle on top of his head.

Blancanales turned to Lyons. "You ever wonder what makes him tick, Carl?" he asked, shaking his head.

The Able Team Leader nodded. "Constantly."

Schwarz opened the door and slid into the back seat. "Well, how do you like it?"

"What is it?" Blancanales returned.

"You've never seen a cowboy hat before, Pol?" Schwarz asked, irritated. "Remind me to take you to a John Wayne movie sometime."

Lyons pulled away from the curb and started through town.

"I've *seen* cowboy hats, Gadgets," Blancanales said. "I just never saw one that looked like it cost $1.49 before."

Schwarz pulled the hat from his head and dropped it on the seat next to him. "Hey, I had to do something," he said. "As long as you guys took, people were beginning to notice me. I figured I'd better become a tourist."

"How much did it cost?" Blancanales asked.

Schwarz mumbled something under his breath.

"Couldn't hear you, Gadgets," Pol said.

"Forty-five dollars."

Blancanales hooked a thumb back toward the old men in front of the Irma. "Next time take out your knife and grab a piece of wood like the rest of the good ol' boys. It'll be cheaper, and who knows, you might make some new friends."

"I was trying not to stand out, remember?" Schwarz reached inside his leather jacket and produced the long blade of an SOG Pentagon. "This is hardly your average whittler."

Lyons followed the highway west, out of town. Five miles after the last buildings had disappeared on the horizon, he spotted a grove of trees at the end of a side road, turned off and parked the Blazer out of sight as the sun began to fall behind the mountains.

Killing the ignition, the Able Team leader rested an arm over the seat and turned toward Schwarz. "One-story brick house, upper-middle-class residential neighborhood," he said. "Front and rear entrances. Windows on all sides."

Schwarz nodded. "See any of the bad guys?"

"Just one. Uzi. But there'll be more." Lyons paused. "I'll take the front door. Gadgets, you've got the rear. Pol, I want you outside. Go to the back and watch the windows on both sides."

Both Schwarz and Blancanales nodded.

"Any questions?" Lyons asked.

"Can I wear my new hat?"

"No."

Schwarz remained deadpan as he shrugged. Blancanales laughed and shook his head again.

"Let's get ready," Lyons said, opening the door. He walked to the rear of the Blazer, swung the tire rack back and unlocked the gate. A moment later, Pol and Gadgets were unloading various boxes and cases.

The three men of Able Team tossed their street clothes into the empty containers and began donning their blacksuits. Lyons shrugged back into the new shoulder rig, positioning it over the stretchy black combat suit and tying it down around the gun belt that held his Python, speed-loaders and extra magazines for the Gold Cup.

Schwarz and Blancanales each carried a 9 mm Beretta 92-F. Gadgets backed up his auto with a tiny 7-shot Firestar .45ACP, while Blancanales had chosen what might well be the most unusual weapon off the assembly line in years: the Thunder Five.

"Any man who carries something like that should watch what he says about funny hats," Schwarz cracked as Pol slipped the odd-looking 5-shot revolver into the holster on his hip. "What's it shoot?"

"You got your choice, Gadgets," Blancanales said. "Either .410 shot or .45 long Colt. I've got shotgun shells in it, and two speed-loaders full of .45 that Cowboy rigged up for me." He patted a large nylon pouch around his waist.

Lyons knelt on the cool mountain ground and unlocked a long metal chest. Raising the lid, he reached in and pulled out the first of the three Calico M 961 A concealable submachine guns. He handed it over his shoulder to Blancanales, then gave the second subgun to Schwarz, keeping the third for himself.

Gadgets had already pulled the three shoulder rigs from another bag. The Able Team leader slipped his arms into his, careful that the extra 100-round backup drum hung below and out of the way of the Gold Cup holstered under his left arm.

Slipping into the wraparound-headset walkie-talkies, the Stony Man warriors reloaded the suitcases and got back into the Blazer. They left the grove of trees and headed back toward Cody as darkness fell over the Rockies.

The lights were on in the front of the house as Lyons made a recon pass in the front of Gilbert Watson's house. He parked a block away, and the three men shrugged into light raincoats to cover their weapons during the short walk back.

Two doors away, Schwarz broke off and ducked between a two-story brick house and a split-level structure covered with aluminum siding. Lyons and Blancanales broke into a jog as they crossed Watson's front yard. Pol headed around the side of the house as Lyons shrugged out of his raincoat, vaulting the two steps onto the front porch.

The Able Team leader didn't break stride as he raised his right foot and snapped it out against the door. As the lock broke, he swung the Calico to the end of the sling and shouldered his way into the house.

A half-dozing man in a tight white T-shirt and jeans sat on the floor against the wall of the entryway. He dived for the M-16 A-1 leaning next to him, getting his hand on the pistol grip as Lyons swung the subgun his way.

A split second before he squeezed the trigger, Schwarz entered the rear of the house. The Able Team leader turned his attention back to the man on the floor, cutting loose with a full-auto burst of 9 mm semijacketed hollowpoints that stuttered from the Calico's barrel at 700 rounds per minute. The empty brass blew down out of the ejection port, bouncing on the thick carpet around Lyons's feet.

Both 9 mm Calico bullets and .223 rifle rounds exploded from the back of the house as the man in the jeans fell back against the wall, then slid to his side on the floor.

Lyons stopped, taking in the floor plan. Straight ahead, beyond the foyer, a hallway led to the rear of the house. From where he stood, he could just see the corner of a green felt-covered pool table. That room would be to Gadgets's right, and the Able Team electronics man would head that way.

To his own right, Lyons saw a formal living room, and beyond the living room, what appeared to be a dining area. He pivoted on the balls of his feet, the Calico raised to shoulder level as he burst under an archway and scanned the couches and chairs.

The living room was empty.

A sixth sense suddenly raised the hair on the former cop's nape. He dropped low, twisting at the hip, as a sudden explosion from the rear threatened to deafen him.

A blast of 12-gauge buckshot sailed over Lyons's head and shoulders as he turned to see a muscular man in a blue chambray shirt work the slide of a Mossburg 500. The slide moved forward, chambering another shell, as Lyons tapped the Calico's trigger again.

The 7-round burst started just above the man's crotch, worked its way up the chambray shirt, then into the shotgunner's neck. His bottom lip fell open, blood dripping from his mouth as he tumbled headfirst to the floor.

Lyons swept the area for more of Watson's guards, then turned back toward the dining room through another archway. He moved cautiously forward, staring straight ahead, relying on his peripheral vision to cover the corners on both sides of the arch.

The fire from the rear of the house had moved. Gadgets had worked his way into the pool room.

Lyons stopped five feet from the dining room. Ahead, he saw a blond oak dining table and matching chairs. The room looked as empty as the living room, but gunners could be hidden behind either or both of the short walls that formed the archway.

It was a no-win situation. Regardless of which side he stuck his head around first, if the enemy lay behind the other wall, the Able Team leader would be dead.

Lyons did the only reasonable thing.

Lifting the Calico to eye-level, he aligned the sights on top of the drum. The high-tech subgun spit a steady stream of relentless fire into the arch wall to his right, as Lyons drew an *S* in the white wallboard. Dust, paper and chips of gypsum flew through the air as he reversed the curve, turning the *S* into an *8*.

A man wearing light black denim shirt and white tie fell out from behind cover, the Uzi in his fists clattering to the floor.

Lyons had no time to congratulate himself.

The man behind the other arch wall had seen what had happened and knew it was time to play his hand. Stepping to the side of the wall, he used the wooden trim to steady his aim as he fired another Uzi from the barricade position.

Lyons swung the Calico his way.

The Able Team leader cut another *S* in the thin wallboard, dropping the gunner.

Hearing footsteps behind him, Lyons pivoted.

The Calico's sights fell on Schwarz. Able Team's electronics man was pushing Gilbert Watson forward. The counterfeiter tripped, sprawling in a heap on the floor of the living room.

"Everything clear?" Lyons queried.

"Affirmative. Van Gogh gave up without a fight. Their gear is set up in the pool room."

"Let's go look." Lyons flipped a switch, then spoke into the mouthpiece of the walkie-talkie. "Able One to Two," he said. "Anybody get out of the house, Pol?"

"Negative. How come you guys always get to have all the fun?"

"Come on in," Lyons replied. "On the double. We've got to get samples and get out of here before the cops show up. The neighbors are bound to have called in."

Lyons leaned down, hauling Gilbert Watson to his feet by the ear. The counterfeiter roared as the Able Team leader dragged him out of the dining room, followed by Schwarz.

One man, wearing a gray T-shirt and blue jeans, lay in a pool of blood next to the refrigerator in the kitchen. Lyons stepped over him, hauling Watson into the pool room where the last two of the counterfeiter's guards had fallen to Schwarz's Calico. Blancanales arrived a moment later.

Beyond the pool table, set against the wall, Lyons saw the huge multilift printing press. Next to it stood a plate camera. Twenty-four-inch plates, a vacuum table, photographic negatives and other equipment of Van Gogh's "art" were scattered about the room; and the pool table, Lyons saw now, had been converted to a storage table.

Sticking out of several cardboard boxes against a side wall was the art itself.

Lyons turned to Gilbert Watson. "Who are you working for?" the Able Team leader demanded.

Watson's eyeglasses had fallen over the bridge of his nose. He looked over them, a quizzical expression on his face. "Working for? What do you mean, working for?"

Lyons started to reach for him but Schwarz held up a hand. "Please, Ironman. I've been waiting all night for this line."

He poked the counterfeiter in the chest. "Elementary, my dear Watson." Watson's glasses flew to the floor. Schwarz's voice became a low menacing growl. "Who are you making these bills for?"

Watson blinked his eyes, then said, "But...I work for myself. I've always been on my own...." His voice trailed off as a police siren sounded in the distance.

"We've got to get out of here," Lyons said. "Gadgets, grab one of those boxes of funny money."

Schwarz moved toward the boxes as Blancanales stepped forward. "What do we do with him?" He nodded toward Watson.

Watson answered the question for him.

As Lyons turned toward the man, one of the pudgy counterfeiter's hands ripped open his shirt. The other shot inside as the elastic material of a belly-band holster appeared, wedged into a roll of hairy fat.

The Able Team leader started to bring his Calico into play as Watson drew a Smith & Wesson Chief

Special from the elastic. He stopped as a deafening blast exploded next to him.

The counterfeiter's .38 fell from his fingers.

Lyons turned to his side in time to see Blancanales holstering the Thunder Five .410 pistol.

The sirens were louder as Carl Lyons flipped the Calico's selector back onto "safe" and led his teammates into the kitchen and out the back door.

Stony Man Farm

AARON KURTZMAN RUBBED the stubble of beard on his left cheek. He hadn't had time to shave for two days now, and it looked like he wouldn't get the opportunity this day, either. Unless a miracle happened.

Kurtzman's hand moved to the other cheek. Not that he didn't believe in miracles; he did. He saw them all the time around Stony Man Farm. Some of the miracles were created by the skills and training of Mack Bolan. Other wonders were performed by Carl Lyons, Yakov Katzenelenbogen or the other men of Phoenix Force and Able Team. And while the marvels he witnessed might not be quite as mysterious as the parting of the Red Sea, they were miracles nonetheless.

As Kurtzman dropped his hand to the console next to the keyboard, he leaned back in his wheelchair. Who next? he wondered. He glanced to the handwritten list on the console. Beneath the letters *SASR*, he saw *E*, *S* and *I*. Escadron Special D'Intervention—

Special Intervention Squadron. He smiled grimly. "If this is Tuesday, it must be Belgium," he said under his breath.

The intercom buzzed. He lifted the receiver to his ear with one hand as the other began tapping into the files of the ESI, Belgium's top counter-terrorist unit. "Yeah, Barb?"

"Ironman just called in," Price said. "They took down the Watson operation in Cody, but had to get out when the police showed up. They're on their way north to some little town called Powell, just across the Montana line. They'll fax samples of the funny money to you as soon as they're set up."

"Affirmative, Barb," Kurtzman said. He turned toward the glass wall that separated the Computer Room from Mission Control. Price sat at her console, facing him. "Heard from Phoenix Force?"

Price nodded. "That's affirmative," she said into the phone. "They got out fine. They're at a Mossad safehouse with a prisoner. They were about to start interrogating him when Katz called."

The fax machine at the other end of the computer bank began to hum. Kurtzman nodded to Price through the glass, hung up and wheeled himself toward it.

Copies of hundred-dollar bills began kicking out into the tray.

Kurtzman waited until the machine shut off, then lifted the sheaf of papers and wheeled himself back to the computer. Pulling the top page off the stack, he fed it into a slot in the mainframe.

The computer ace tapped several keys on the keyboard, entering into the counterfeit identification program he had designed and programmed into the computer. The computer would make its own photo of the bill, then begin systematically searching for similarities and differences between it and the "hundreds" Able Team had found with the Russian arms shipment in Canada.

Kurtzman sat back, rubbing the stubble on his chin as the computer went to work. Even using faxes, his program was far superior to the counterfeit machines used by the Secret Service. It had readily detected the near-perfect bills that had been recovered earlier. Of course it was limited to visual comparison and couldn't compare paper weight or texture, but Kurtzman knew it would be able to determine whether the bills from Gilbert Watson were linked into the rest of the mission.

The screen lighted up with the answer.

Kurtzman lifted the phone and turned back to Price. "Can you contact Lyons direct?" he asked.

Price nodded. She turned to her console phone and tapped a series of buttons.

A moment later, Kurtzman heard the ring.

"Super 8 Motel, Powell," a male voice stated.

"Mr. Jessup's room, please," Price said.

The desk clerk rang the room.

"Hello?"

"I'm sorry, Ironman," Aaron Kurtzman said without preamble. "But the bills from Cody aren't even close to the ones you guys picked up before."

Dublin, Ireland

THE IRISH QUARTET quit playing. A hush fell over the pub as the explosion from the Huntsman's suicide round died down.

Then a woman's scream broke the silence. Horrified voices followed.

Still holding the Desert Eagle out of sight beneath his jacket, Bolan stepped to the side of the body and started toward the door. He needed a set of the man's fingerprints so Kurtzman could track down the true identity of this new Huntsman. But this was hardly the time or place. The police would arrive shortly, seal off the entrances and begin to question everyone present.

That included the Executioner if he didn't vacate the premises fast.

Bolan had his hand on the doorknob when he heard a gun hammer click back.

"Hold on, chappie."

The Executioner looked over to see a pudgy man in his early fifties training a snubbie Smith & Wesson Model 66 at his chest. The man wore a Donegal tweed sport coat over his crumpled white shirt. The knot of his tie had been pulled down from his throat, and the tie itself sported the spots and stains of many meals.

Everything about the man's appearance shouted off-duty cop.

"Don't you be movin' a muscle," the cop threatened.

Bolan studied the man's face. It was red from drink, but his eyes still focused clearly. His reactions would be slower than usual, but not by much.

The Executioner had never killed a policeman, and he didn't intend to start now. While the cops themselves might not always agree, Bolan saw himself fighting on the same side as law-enforcement officers the world over.

"Now...*slowly*..." the off-duty cop said. "What might it be that you're hiding under your cloak?"

Bolan gauged the distance between the two of them. One fast step would close the gap. He'd be able to rap the heavy Desert Eagle against the man's temple, drop him to the floor and leave him with nothing worse than a headache when he woke up.

If the man's reactions were slow enough. If not, the Executioner would end his career on the floor next to this latest Huntsman. Which would it be?

The warrior never got a chance to find out.

As he started to move, the barrel of another gun jammed into his ribs from behind. "Don't you be playing the fool now, mate," said the unseen man. Then, "Ryan, you got your cuffs with you?"

"No."

"Then I suppose we'll be usin' mine."

A hand reached around the Executioner, fumbled under his coat and relieved him of the Desert Eagle. "Holy Mother of Jesus," the voice said. "The chappie's come to hunt elephants."

The red-faced man moved in, spun Bolan and pushed him against the wall next to the door. The Executioner caught a quick glimpse of the other cop. In his early twenties, he already had the red bulbous nose of a heavy drinker. Ryan shook him down, finding the Beretta, then the extra magazines for both pistols. "And he's come for the whole herd," the Irishman said.

A second later, Bolan felt the cold steel of the handcuffs clamp over his wrists. Ryan turned him back around, then holstered his revolver. "Call it in, Mike," he ordered the younger cop.

The young man headed for the bar.

"Already done" came the voice of the bartender.

A siren sounded outside the pub. A second later, the door burst open and two uniformed men entered, weapons drawn.

"What do you have, Ryan?" asked a gray-haired man wearing sergeant's stripes.

"A suicide, it appeared," Ryan answered. "But the damnedest one I've seen in me twenty-eight years." He nodded toward Bolan. "This bloke's involved somehow, and I mean to find out how." He held up the Beretta and Desert Eagle.

"You'll be taking him to headquarters yourself, then?" the sergeant asked.

Ryan nodded. "McShane and I," he said, indicating the younger man.

The sergeant nodded. He sniffed the air, then grinned. "Best be stoppin' at the chemist's on the way," he suggested.

Ryan nodded, then prodded Bolan toward the door, held open by McShane. Taking a firm grip on the chain linking the Executioner's hands, the tipsy cop tugged upward and guided him out of the pub to the sidewalk.

He pushed Bolan toward a sedan parked down the block. Three antennas rose from the hood and trunk, identifying it as a detective's car. Both men shoved him into the back seat.

"We'll be needin' a story," the younger man said.

"Surveillance on a possible drug transaction," Ryan replied in a practiced voice. "Anonymous tip." He slid into the passenger's seat in front of the Executioner and dropped the Desert Eagle, Beretta and extra magazines on the seat next to him. Leaning across the seat, he slapped the younger man on the knee. "Don't you be worryin', Mikey me boy. It's Johnny Mackleduff wearing the lieutenant bars tonight. He sneaks off for a few quick ones now and again, himself."

So that was it. The two plainclothesmen weren't off duty. They'd simply slipped away long enough to drink. The sergeant back at the pub had known that, and it had prompted the warning about Ryan's breath.

The Executioner knew he had to find a chance to escape before they got to the station. Once there, he'd be delayed for hours—maybe days—until Brognola could pull the necessary strings to get him out. It would take time.

Time the Executioner didn't have.

The unmarked vehicle took off down the street. Six blocks later, Ryan held up a hand and pointed to a pharmacy on the right. "Pull in, Mikey," he said. "I'll be grabbin' some mouthwash and mints."

McShane turned the car into a shadowy corner of a parking lot next to the pharmacy and killed the ignition. His partner got out and disappeared into the building.

Bolan knew it was now or never as he watched McShane's reflection in the mirror. The young cop was paying him little attention, secure in the knowledge that his prisoner was handcuffed.

But that didn't mean that what Bolan was about to do would be easy.

Slowly the Executioner shifted in his seat, turning slightly toward the door. McShane glanced at him in the mirror. "Cuffs too tight?" he asked.

Bolan nodded.

The young detective nodded. "Life's a bitch."

Now that he had the young man used to his movement, Bolan shifted even farther. When his back faced McShane, he took a deep breath, then moved fast.

The warrior's head nearly hit the roof of the car as he rose to his feet. He arched back toward the man behind the wheel, raising his cuffed hands as high as he could, then looping them around the detective's throat.

Bolan tugged the man's head tight against his back and heard the gurgling sound as the oxygen was cut off. The detective's fingers clawed up, raking across the Executioner's back. When the struggling ceased, Bolan let up on the pressure.

McShane didn't move.

Unlooping his bound wrists, Bolan crawled over the front seat backward. McShane's eyes were closed, but the Executioner could see his chest moving up and down with each breath. He breathed a silent sigh of relief.

The difference between a choke that caused a man to lose consciousness and one that took his life was a matter of seconds.

McShane had come close to death. But he'd be all right when he woke up.

Bolan's eyes saw the handcuff key on the key ring in the ignition. Pressing his back against the steering wheel, he reached for it. As he pulled it free, he saw Ryan come out of the pharmacy carrying a small sack.

The warrior slipped the key ring around a thumb, then turned, grabbing the Beretta with his right hand. He dived back over the seat as Ryan reached the car.

The half-sober cop slid in and said, "Let's go."

Bolan worked the handcuff key into his right cuff and twisted. The lock swung free.

"Mike, I said let's—"

The barrel of the Beretta pushing into Ryan's temple cut him off in midsentence.

"Very, *very,* slowly, I want you to hand me your gun," Bolan said.

The detective did as he was told. Bolan swung the cylinder out of the revolver, dumped the .357 hollowpoints on the floor and set it on the seat.

"Now put your hands on the dash."

The red-faced cop leaned forward.

The handcuffs still dangling from his left wrist, the Executioner reached over the seat and retrieved the Desert Eagle and extra magazines. He holstered the Eagle and dropped the mags into the side pockets of his coat.

"You've killed me partner," Ryan stated.

"He's just taking a little nap."

"Then you'll be killing us both now, I suppose," Ryan said in a tone of resignation. He waited for an answer. When he didn't get one, he turned slowly, fearful that each inch he moved would be his last.

To his surprise, the bullet he expected didn't come. And when he had turned far enough to see into the dark back seat, he found it empty.

4

Yakov Katzenelenbogen stared through the windshield of the van. Far in the distance, he saw the towering peak of Mount Tabor, north of Nazareth.

Nazareth, in Galilee, lay just off the main highway that had run though ancient Palestine. By all rights, it should have evolved into a thriving metropolitan area, but it had played only one major role in the history of the region—it had been the boyhood home of Jesus Christ.

Gary Manning, the van's driver, spoke up as they drove into Nazareth and started down one of its narrow winding streets. "Which way?" he asked.

Katz turned toward the rear of the vehicle, where David McCarter sat between Encizo and James. After fingerprinting Jabbar, McCarter had begun a more gentle form of questioning. It had been nothing more than an elaborate variation of the old "Good Cop Bad Cop" technique, which had proved useful to police officers time after time.

McCarter pointed straight ahead. "Stay on this road until you see the Church of the Annunciation. There's a Franciscan monastery just beyond it. Pass it and take a right."

Manning nodded.

"You're sure our Bloody Wind friend was telling the truth?" Katz asked.

"Our Bloody Wind friend bloody well better have been," the Briton said. He looked at James. "Or I'll turn him back over to this Yank demon with the banana knife."

James gritted his teeth, then opened his lips into a crazy demented smile.

The van slowed as it passed the 'Ain-Sitt Miriam, known in the West as "Mary's Well." Katz saw women waiting in line to fill huge earthenware jugs with water, no different than they had done two thousand years earlier.

Katz's mind returned to Jabbar. They had turned the terrorist over to Ranon Goldberg so the Mossad could further interrogate him.

The van passed through a modern retail center, then entered a neighborhood of twenty-year-old houses. Katz noted they were well kept for the most part. When they passed what looked like a school building, McCarter dropped his gaze from the window to the notebook in his lap. "I think that's it," the Briton said. "Jabbar said the building used to be a school." He paused, then asked, "Katz, can you make out the sign?"

The sign was in both Hebrew and Arabic. Katz studied the letters as they drove past. "It's an evaluation center for people with physical disabilities. I assume that disabled people go there to be classified for state disability pensions and such."

"That's it, then. Jabbar said the Bloody Wind boys are in the basement below."

"How have they pulled *that* off?" Manning wondered.

Katz shrugged. "Payoffs. Maybe a sympathizer in the power seat. Who knows? The point is, they've done it."

"So," Encizo asked, "any ideas how we get in and correct it? They're bound to have lookouts upstairs. Five guys with no outward signs of disability are going to turn a few heads."

Yakov Katzenelenbogen hadn't spoken since they'd passed the building. He'd been too busy unlacing his prosthetic right arm. Now, as the van turned the corner again, he pulled the lace through the last loop. Jerking the artificial limb from the stump under his shirt, he handed it between the seats to McCarter. "Look after this for me."

"Certainly," McCarter said. Then straight-faced, he added, "I can always count on you to give me a hand, Katz."

Then, the Israeli turned to Manning. "Drop me off at the corner. We're about to find out just how much I could make by not working."

"Going on the dole, are you?" McCarter asked in the same dry voice.

"No, on the prowl," Katz replied as Manning pulled the van to the curb. He shrugged out of his shoulder holster and dropped it on the seat. "Be ready to roll as soon as you see me come out." He opened the door.

McCarter cleared his throat and Katz looked back.

"Something else?" the Phoenix Force leader asked.

McCarter's face was deadpan as he held up the prosthetic limb. "I just wanted to say I'm touched, Katz," he said, wiping an imaginary tear from the corner of his eye. "I've always heard you'd give your right arm for your men. Now I know it's true."

Deadwood, South Dakota

THE BLACK HILLS of South Dakota had seen more than their share of lawlessness during the frontier mining days of the 1800s. For a dozen years, outlaws had ridden the mountains and canyons with near impunity, raping, robbing, looting and burning. Among the prospectors were former marshals and sheriffs, but they had been far more interested in panning gold than wearing it on their chests.

Law and order had come slowly. And never completely.

The legacy of Deadwood, written on the faded tombstones of Mount Moriah Cemetery, lay in the names: Calamity Jane Burk, Potato Creek Johnny, Seth Bullock, Preacher Smith. And of course, James Butler "Wild Bill" Hickok.

Carl Lyons sat facing the door of the Number 10 Saloon on Main Street. Outside the open door, a dozen motorcycles raced by, followed by several cars. The timing was wrong for the yearly Harley Davidson run in nearby Sturgis, when two hundred thousand leather-clad men and women would descend on the Black Hills. But Lyons knew that the area was rarely without a few hundred men and women in black leather astride bikes. Most were simple, honest, hardworking citizens who liked to ride motorcycles and partied hard. But a few—one percent by their own calculations—were modern-day versions of Jesse James, Cole Younger and Bill Dalton.

Across from Lyons, wearing his black leather motorcycle jacket and looking as if he himself had been born on a Harley, sat Gadgets Schwarz. At the bar, waiting for the bartender, Rosario Blancanales still wore the denim pullover.

All three Able Team warriors were working hard not to stand out in a crowd during their search for known counterfeiters. Deadwood was a lot like Cody—small. Local criminals knew local cops personally, and word of any new "cop-looking" faces would get around fast.

Schwarz looked at his watch, then Lyons. "What's the name of the guy we're supposed to be meeting?" he asked.

"Jenkins," Lyons replied. "Special Agent Nathan Jenkins."

Schwarz nodded. "You sure he said Number 10 Saloon? He's almost an hour late. I've never known a G-man that didn't ask how high when Hal said jump."

Lyons nodded as Blancanales returned with three beer mugs. "Jenkins said Saloon Number 10—where Wild Bill Hickok got shot." He took a sip of beer, then set the mug down next to a discarded tourist brochure on the tabletop. "But you're right—something's wrong. We'll give it five more minutes, then call in." He watched Blancanales take a seat next to Schwarz and pick up the brochure.

A moment later, Able Team's ace undercover and psychological warfare man frowned. "Well, I've got some good news and some bad news."

Lyons and Schwarz waited.

"According to this," Blancanales said, tapping the brochure with an index finger, "Wild Bill was shot in the *original* Saloon Number 10, which is now the Eagle Bar. Down the street."

Lyons muttered under his breath as the three men stood and hurried out the door. Justice agents were supposed to be professionals, and part of that professionalism was the ability to pick a meeting site that couldn't get confused. If that proved impossible, they at least explained the fact that there could be confusion ahead of time.

The Able Team leader led the way into the Eagle Bar, then stopped. The usual slot machines and blackjack tables circled the room. A mustachioed dummy swung from the ceiling, a noose around his neck. A sign pointed downstairs, announcing the exact spot where Wild Bill had supposedly been killed.

Scouting the patrons, Lyons saw perhaps two dozen leather-clad bikers and the usual assortment of men and women in tourist garb, complete with cameras. Alone, at a table in the corner, sat a balding man wearing a gray three-piece suit.

"Now I wonder which one might be Jenkins?" Schwarz said sarcastically. He turned to Lyons, and the Able Team leader saw Gadgets's face flushed with anger. "You know, Ironman, we went to a lot of trouble to blend in here. Now this jerk comes in looking like a cross between Elliot Ness and J. Edgar Hoover and blows it all. I ought to—"

"Okay," Lyons cut him off. "It's too late to do anything about it now. Let's just get the meeting over, ditch him and get on with it." He led the way to the table.

The man in the gray suit stood and extended his hand as they approached. "Special Agent Nathan Jenkins, Department of Justice," he said, loud enough to make several heads turn. "What took you so—"

Lyons grabbed the man's shoulder and shoved him back down in his chair. Jenkins's face became of mask of surprise and embarrassment.

"Done much undercover work, Jenkins?" Lyons asked.

"Why, no."

"Done much work, period?" Schwarz asked.

"Let's get out of here," Lyons said, glancing around to see that half the bar had stopped talking and was now watching them. "Jenkins, you follow us. Stay at least ten feet behind."

"If you can count to ten," Schwarz said as he and Blancanales followed Lyons out of the bar.

Pol led the way to the Blazer parked at the end of the block. "You think he's blown it?" he asked.

"Not yet," Lyons replied. "But an hour from now every bad boy in the Black Hills is going to know that there's four new Feds around, and they're going to know that three of them were trying to dress like tourists. Dope's going to get flushed down the toilet, and illegal weapons are going to be buried." He drew a disgusted breath. "It wouldn't surprise me if anybody in the counterfeiting business didn't start packing, too." They reached the Blazer. "Which means we've got to locate our man fast."

Schwarz opened the back door and turned around in time to see Nathan Jenkins come to a halt. "Get in," the electronics man ordered.

Jenkins did as he was told.

Lyons waited until Schwarz had gotten in beside him and Blancanales had taken the shotgun spot before sliding behind the wheel. He turned toward the back seat. "Due to the time element you've created, Jenkins," he said, "I'm going to spare you the lecture I had planned. But Brognola's going to hear about this. You might want to pack for a long tour of duty somewhere north of Barstow, Alaska.'' He cleared his throat. "Did you get Cary Gamble's address?"

The man in the gray suit was in minor shock as he reached into his jacket pocket and pulled out a slip of paper. "Here it is. But I'll tell you the same thing I told Mr. Brognola. We don't have anything on Mr. Gamble. As far as we can tell, he's been clean since he was released from the penitentiary last year. Your information must be incorrect.''

Lyons felt the anger begin to swell inside him. His chest felt like a rumbling volcano that might explode any second and take the top of his head with it. Not only was Jenkins a paper-pushing incompetent, he was now trying the old bureaucratic trick of shifting the blame, never admitting to a mistake.

Blancanales came to Jenkins's rescue. "You'd better get out, now,'' he told the G-man.

"No, I've been given orders to go along with you. I—''

"Nathan,'' Schwarz said softly, taking the agent's elbow and nodding toward Lyons. "Take a good look at this man's face.''

Jenkins turned to Lyons, and the skin around his eyes went white.

"Believe me,'' Schwarz said. "You should get out now.''

Blancanales leaned over the seat, found the handle and swung the door open.

"So long, Special Agent Jenkins of the U.S. Department of Justice," Schwarz said and shouldered the man out of the vehicle.

Jenkins fell to a sitting position on the sidewalk.

The Justice agent had a look of dazed confusion on his face as the Blazer pulled away from the curb.

Dublin, Ireland

IT HAPPENED FAST—so fast that cabbie Willie O'Hara had only a hazy recollection to report to police later.

One moment O'Hara was sitting behind the wheel, parked in front of the Shelbourne in downtown Dublin, waiting for the late-night fare that had called in from the first-class hotel. He had downed three glasses of ale and a shepherd's pie an hour or so ago. He was still sleepy, and as he waited, he'd lapsed into an alcohol-induced half dream.

The dream was filled with hands, soft feminine hands that did pleasant things to his body. The faces above the hands smiled down at him as they worked, and belonged to two well-known movie stars and the wife of his next-door neighbor. Willie drifted in the feelings they produced, and for a split second he thought that the hands that ripped the driver's-side door open were part of the dream.

The misconception didn't last long.

As he hit the grass of Saint Stephen's Green, O'Hara realized that the hands that had wrenched him from the cab were big, strong and masculine. And while they didn't really seem to be trying to hurt him, they were intent on getting him out of the vehicle as quickly and efficiently as possible. As he sat there on the grass trying to get his bearings, one of the big hands came back and ripped the leather cap off his head.

It was then that O'Hara came out of the dream completely and sobered up fast.

A second later, the cab had pulled away. O'Hara was left wondering exactly what had been real, and what had been a figment of his imagination.

So Willie O'Hara decided that rather than replace the cap the big hands had taken, he'd buy a few more glasses of ale with the ten-pound note the stranger had left.

BOLAN TOOK the first corner past the Shelbourne and headed back toward the Culturalann na hEireann. His foot fell heavy on the accelerator as he dropped the leather cap on his head. He knew he was fighting time. It would be a race against the clock to see if he could get back to the pub before the police took the body away.

Bolan slowed slightly as he approached an intersection. He had to get a set of fingerprints from the body to Kurtzman for identification. That meant that if the body had already been removed, he'd have to find the morgue, then figure an angle into the building before the autopsy that would probably be done the next morning. All that would take time, and during that time, more might die to the Huntsman.

The Executioner slowed again as he saw the flashing lights a block ahead. Tugging the visor of the cap lower on his forehead, he pulled into a parallel parking space three storefronts from the pub and killed the engine.

Two marked police units stood in front of the pub. The sidewalk was crowded with curious onlookers, and several uniformed men were holding them back, their truncheons grasped in both hands.

Bolan settled back against the seat and waited. He knew it was merely a matter of time before word got back to the pub that he'd escaped custody. But the Dublin cops wouldn't be looking for a cab, and certainly they wouldn't expect him to come back to the Culturalann.

Five minutes later, an ambulance pulled up in front of the pub. Two young men in the uniforms of medical technicians got out. An officer escorted them inside.

The two med-techs returned a few minutes later bearing the stretcher between them. A zippered body bag lay on top of the canvas straps.

The same cop who had taken them into the pub opened the back of the ambulance and helped them slide the body inside. A moment later they pulled away.

The Executioner fell in behind, turning his face away from the cops on the sidewalk as he passed the pub. He let the cab fall a block behind the ambulance as he followed it around a corner and up a ramp onto a crosstown thoroughfare.

Bolan watched the taillights of the vehicle as he increased speed. Somewhere along the line, he had to find a way to stop the ambulance. What he wanted wouldn't take long to get, but he had to get it before they reached the morgue. Otherwise, he'd waste half the night figuring out a way into the building.

The ambulance slowed as it passed a sign announcing the O'Connell Street exit. Bolan followed, hoping against hope that the men ahead would lead him down a dark street before they reached the morgue.

It wasn't to be.

The traffic on O'Connell was like Hollywood Boulevard on Saturday night, and the street seemed only slightly less bright as the Executioner followed the ambulance down Dublin's principal road. They passed shops, banks, travel bureaus and hotels, most closed for the night but all boasting high-security lighting.

The idea came to the Executioner quickly. Just as quickly he calculated its pros and cons, then made his decision.

As they passed the General Post Office and entered a line of government buildings, Bolan twisted the wheel of the cab, hit the accelerator, pulled into the passing lane and drew abreast of the ambulance. He honked the horn once as he cut in front of the ambulance.

The rear fender of the cab scraped the front of the other vehicle, and a piece of grillwork clattered to the concrete.

The Executioner glanced into the rearview mirror. He couldn't hear what the man driving the ambulance was saying, but the shaking fist told him he was far from happy.

Slowing, Bolan pulled into the next driveway and drove to the parking lot of a yellow brick building. The ambulance followed.

The Executioner jerked the cap from his head as he got out of the cab, holding it meekly in front of him as he walked back toward the ambulance.

"You bloody fool!" the driver yelled as he got out of the vehicle. "You damn near killed—"

The voice stopped abruptly as Bolan lowered the cap long enough for the man to see the .44 Magnum Desert Eagle hidden behind it. Replacing the cap in front of the gun, he stepped up to the man. "Get back in the ambulance, do what you're told and you might live through the night."

The driver nodded and got back behind the wheel.

Bolan opened the door to the back seat and got in, training the .44 toward the front. "Gentlemen," he said, "I don't want much, and what I do want won't take long if you cooperate. If you don't cooperate, it'll take a little longer but I'll still get it. And when I'm finished, you'll be dead."

The man in the passenger's seat had short, curly hair. He started to speak, thought better of it and nodded.

"Give me a pen," Bolan ordered.

The driver reached up, jerked a pen from his shirt pocket and handed it over the seat.

"Now I want a clean white piece of paper."

The curly-headed man leaned toward the floor.

"Careful," Bolan warned as he cocked the Desert Eagle.

The man's movements slowed as he brought up a briefcase and placed it on the seat between him and his partner. Pulling out a spiral notebook, he opened it. "I'm sorry," he said, his voice shaking. "It's got lines. I could go—"

"It'll do," the Executioner said.

The man tore a blank page from the notebook and handed it over the seat.

Bolan took the page, then scooted up over the seat behind him. He kept one eye on the two men in front as he crawled over the body in the back.

Transferring the big .44 to his left hand, the Executioner unzipped the body bag to the waist. He pulled the corpse's hands from the opening and turned them palm-up.

"What are you doing?" the driver blurted out.

Bolan glanced up, his gaze locking with the other man's.

Then the driver turned away and didn't speak again.

Quickly the Executioner unscrewed the fountain pen and broke the ink cartridge he found inside. He let the ink drip into a small pool on the exposed chest of the dead man, then one by one, he dipped the lifeless fingers into the ink.

Using the unlined top margin of the sheet of notebook paper, Bolan carefully rolled a set of prints from the man's right hand. He dropped to the bottom margin and did the same with the left.

When he'd finished, the Executioner crawled back over the seat and tapped the Desert Eagle on top of the driver's head.

The man's voice shook as he said, "Yes—?"

"Give me the keys."

The driver froze. His partner nodded, reached over and pulled the key ring from the ignition.

Bolan pocketed the keys and stepped out of the ambulance, the page with the damp prints held carefully to his side. Opening the door to the cab, he set the paper carefully on the passenger's seat, then reached back into his coat.

The keys to the ambulance sparkled under the bright O'Connell Street lights as they sailed up into the air, then disappeared onto the roof of a nearby building.

Stony Man Farm

BARBARA PRICE HEARD the fax machine kick on and swiveled in her chair to face it.

A moment later, what appeared to be a lined page of notebook paper came out of the machine. At the top of the page, above the first line, the Stony Man mission controller saw five skillfully rolled fingerprint impressions. At the bottom of the page beneath the last line, were five more.

Only two words accompanied the prints. *Right,* stood out at the top of the page. Just above the last line, Price saw *Left.* The words meant right and left hands, of course, but the handwriting itself told her everything else she needed to know about the communication.

The scrawled words were in the handwriting of the Executioner.

Price lifted the phone, tapped Kurtzman's intercom button, then turned toward the glass. "Got another set of prints for you, Bear," she said as the man stopped typing long enough to lift the receiver next to him. "From Striker."

"Let's have them," Kurtzman told her and hung up.

She watched the Stony Man computer genius return to work as she walked toward the door separating their areas. No rookie with computers herself, she was nevertheless always in awe at the dances Kurtzman could cause his magic machines to perform. The man's skill went beyond mere knowledge and technique to combine science with art. Price sometimes wondered where the computer stopped and Aaron Kurtzman, the man, began.

Price climbed to the top of the ramp and took a position behind and slightly to one side of Kurtzman. She waited as Kurtzman tapped several keys, then sat back and watched a file appear on the screen.

"Who's business you into now?" she asked.

"Egypt."

"Why?"

"Sort of a wild hare that went nowhere. They've got even less on the Huntsman deal than the rest of the world—didn't even know about the bottle caps." He leaned forward, typing again, and the screen went black. He twirled in his chair. "Got 'em?" Price handed him the fax.

Kurtzman turned back, set the prints in his lap and frowned down at them. "They haven't been classified yet?"

"They just came in."

He wheeled back from the console and rolled along the bank of computers toward a small box two spaces down. The instrument looked similar to a copy machine, but Price knew it was much more. Designed and built by Kurtzman himself, as far as the mission controller knew there was not another device like it in the world.

Kurtzman opened the cover over the top, dropped the prints onto a clear plastic window and replaced the cover. He flipped a switch and the machine began to hum. As it warmed up, he wheeled back to the computer.

A short buzz sounded from the machine behind him as Kurtzman took his place at the keyboard again. He tapped several commands, and suddenly the screen lighted up with a long fingerprint classification.

"Amazing, Bear," Price said. "You just show the computer a set of the prints and it classifies them for you?"

"Wait," he said, grinning. "It gets better." His fingers flew across the keyboard again. When he'd finished, he sat back and said, "If I had any sense I'd blow this one-horse outfit, take my new invention and patent it. Then I'd take the money, move to Tahiti and drink gin with topless native girls for the rest of my life."

Price laughed as the computer clicked and hummed. Kurtzman held up a hand suddenly as the screen lighted up. "Hold it. I just linked us into AFIS."

Price watched as Kurtzman began entering the print classification into the Automated Fingerprint Identification System. A relatively new setup, AFIS had changed movie and television fantasy into reality. For decades, the general public had held the misconception that a latent fingerprint discovered at the scene of a crime spelled doom for the perpetrator, not realizing that unless there was a suspect to compare to the print, it was of very little value.

Millions of fingerprints were on file throughout the United States, and the human resources to search them all by hand simply didn't exist.

Price grinned as the AFIS system searched the main file and began kicking out the names of the most likely candidates. The computer would narrow a search involving millions down to five or ten of the most likely human beings.

Science fiction had finally become science.

Six potential matchups appeared in the orange lights. Kurtzman tapped in the command to divide the screen and brought up the prints from Dublin in the right window. The names and fingerprint classifications of the six "possible" stayed on the left.

Three minutes later, five of the six names had disappeared. *Chester Gregory Fischbeck, Eugene, Oregon,* still flashed opposite the Dublin prints.

"It's him," Kurtzman said excitedly. "Let's find out a little bit more about Mr. Fischbeck. Such as why he was arrested and fingerprinted." Opening still another window toward the bottom of the screen, the Stony Man computer ace linked into the Eugene PD computer files.

Price watched Kurtzman's smile fade as an EPD file appeared on the screen. He squinted at the orange letters in front of him. "He wasn't arrested," he said. "His prints are on file for employment."

"He was a cop?" Price leaned over Kurtzman's shoulder, scanning down the personnel file. Yes, Fischbeck had been a Eugene PD sergeant. But he had resigned under duress over a police brutality complaint nearly seven years earlier.

Kurtzman tapped the cursor, moving down the screen. "He went to work in the private security field," he said out loud as Price read along. Then the computer whiz's mouth fell open as they both moved to the last paragraph of the file.

"Bear, could it be a mistake?" Price asked as Kurtzman turned to face her in the wheelchair. "Could you have mismatched the prints?"

"I could have, but I didn't."

"So what does it mean?"

Kurtzman looked up into the mission controller's face, his own reflecting a thousand questions. "It means, Barb, that the Huntsman who just killed himself in Dublin *was* Chester Gregory Fischbeck. Fischbeck was an ex-cop. Nobody likes to hear about a cop going bad, but it happens, and people like you and me know that."

He paused, then added, "The part we're having a little trouble with, is how in the hell Fischbeck killed himself in Dublin, Ireland, five years after he died in Monaco."

5

Nazereth, Israel

The front hall of the Physical Disability Evaluation Center was visible through the open double doors as Katz approached. The hall had been turned into a waiting area, and in the chairs against the wall, Katz saw perhaps two dozen dispirited people waiting their turns. Canes, crutches and similar devices had been propped against the wall, but the eyes of their owners were downcast.

A man in a brown corduroy cap, sitting next to the door, caught Katz's attention as he neared the front steps. His eyes darted right, then left, then right again. He appeared to be the only one interested in his surroundings.

Instincts honed in countless missions spawned a last-second decision in the Phoenix Force leader as he reached the steps. Glancing abruptly at his watch as if he'd just remembered something, he changed courses and started toward the side of the building.

Katz knew he needed to find the most direct route to the basement where the Bloody Wind terrorists had holed up. And the people waiting in the hallway for an evaluation of their disabilities hardly looked to have the run of the building. No, they were obviously kept near the front for a reason—and that reason had to be that the basement entrance was located at the rear.

The Stony Man warrior knew he'd learn nothing by sitting in the hall with the other disabled men and women. He needed another way of checking the place out. And at the moment the only ticket he could think of was the tried-and-true "I got lost" story.

He reached the corner of the building and stepped off the sidewalk into a parking lot. Walking past cars he assumed belonged to the social workers and doctors inside, he headed toward the rear of the one-story redbrick structure. The edifice had all the earmarks of having formerly been a grade school, and toward the back of the parking lot he saw a closed steel door.

Katz walked nonchalantly toward the door and pulled on the handle. Locked. He had turned and started away when the squeaking sounds of unoiled wheels on the other side of the door stopped him in his tracks. He stepped to one side as the door opened.

A man in gray work clothes backed through the opening, cursing in Hebrew. Katz saw that he was trying to balance the front of a dolly loaded with boxes. An unseen man—pushing the dolly from the other side, Katz assumed—answered the hard words with profanities of his own.

"Here," Katz said, stepping forward and grabbing the door, "let me help you."

The man pulling the dolly twisted toward him and nodded. Katz held the door as the two men struggled the boxes over the rubber doorjamb onto the parking lot.

Righting the dolly, they both stepped back to catch their breath. The man who had nodded to Katz pulled a handkerchief from his pants and mopped his forehead. "Thank you," he said in Hebrew.

Katz nodded and smiled. "Do not mention it," he replied. He held up the stump of his right arm. "Just do not ask me to open more than one door at a time."

The two workmen hesitated, then burst into laughter as they saw that Katz had meant it as a joke. The Phoenix Force leader joined with a chuckle, then before they had time to question his presence, slid through the door and closed it behind him.

Katz found himself in a semilit rear hallway, which intersected with another just ahead. Unless he missed his guess, this would be the hallway that led back to the front door. Creeping along, he passed several large rooms that had once held students. The glass windows in the doors assured him the classrooms were empty.

The Phoenix Force leader came to the intersecting hallway and stopped, peering slowly around the side. As he had suspected, he saw the front of the building and the other end of the hallway he had already observed from the front door. The same weary people sat in the chairs.

Katz moved back around the corner. All of the evaluation activity had been crowded into the front of the building while the rear classrooms—any of which could have provided a more comfortable waiting area than the hall—sat empty. Whoever was in charge was either a member of Bloody Wind or had been paid off.

Staring into the half-light, Katz squinted across the intersecting hall to the doors on the other side. More empty classrooms, no doubt. Perhaps toilet facilities.

And somewhere, a staircase to the basement.

Quickly he stepped out from the corner and started across the adjoining hall.

He was halfway there when a door ten feet away opened and a woman on crutches stepped out. Behind her, holding the door, stood a short chubby man in shirtsleeves and a tie.

"Thank you for coming, Mrs. Schorr. You will be notified of the results...." The voice trailed off, then "Hey!" echoed down the hall.

Katz kept walking, disappearing behind the next corner as he heard footsteps hurry out into the hall. He quickened his pace slightly, glancing at the doors and windows of more offices as he passed. A door to his right caught his eye. Unlike the other doors, it had no window. That had to be it.

The footsteps rounded the corner and someone yelled again.

Katz turned quickly toward the voice. "You are addressing me?" he asked in Hebrew.

The man in the white shirt and tie walked importantly forward. "Who are you?" he demanded, puffing his chest and jutting out his chin.

Katz laughed in embarrassment. "Samuel Wilenzeck. I was sent for evaluation."

"Why are you in this part of the building? It is restricted."

"I am sorry. I got lost, I suppose."

Suspicion covered the little man's face. "How can you become lost in a building so simple?" he demanded. "Did you not see the people waiting as you came in?"

Katz shrugged. "My friend dropped me off in the parking lot and I came in the side door."

"Impossible. It is kept locked."

Katz shrugged again. "Two workmen were leaving as I got here. I helped them with the door. How was I supposed to know not to enter?"

The man's eyes softened somewhat. "Come this way," he ordered, doing an about-face. "There are forms you must fill out." He led the way toward the front of the building. Pointing toward the chairs against the wall, he stepped up to the reception window and lifted a pad of light blue forms.

Katz took a seat between a woman in a wheelchair and the man in the corduroy cap. Again, the man in the cap seemed to be the only one of the waiting people to notice him. His coal-black eyes stared straight ahead, but Katz could feel himself being scrutinized.

A Bloody Wind lookout? Perhaps. The man had no obvious disability. Of course that meant little. But it seemed reasonable that the terrorists would station someone at the front door to give advance warning in case they were discovered.

A moment later, the chubby administrator returned holding one of the blue forms. "This must be filled out properly," he said. "When you have finished, give it to the woman at the window and return to your seat. You will be called when it is your turn." He started to turn away, then turned back. "Do not wander around the building on your own," he ordered. "Is that clear?"

"As crystal." Katz smiled. "Once again, I am sorry."

The man walked down the hall and disappeared into the same door from which he had emerged.

Katz glanced down the questions on the form. It looked like a good half hour job, and it gave him the excuse he needed. Turning to the man in the corduroy cap, he said, "Why should I do this here when I can go home, then bring it back, right?"

The man in the cap shrugged.

Yakov Katzenelenbogen rose and left the building.

Deadwood, South Dakota

THE TWO-STORY VICTORIAN house six blocks from downtown Deadwood appeared to be in contradiction of itself. Laid back, quiet and dark, it nevertheless had at least two dozen Harley-Davidson motorcycles parked in the driveway and front yard.

"Is Cary Gamble a biker, Ironman?" Schwarz asked as Lyons drove the Blazer past the house. In addition to the bikes, three panel vans stood out front.

Lyons shook his head. "No. And that's not the kind of thing that gets left out of Intel reports."

"How old is he?" Blancanales asked.

"Mid-forties."

Schwarz laughed. "Then this biker thing is either part of a mid-life crisis, or else he's just hired a bunch of cycle jocks to cover his ass while he prints his money."

"My guess is behind door number two," Blancanales said. "Gamble's one of the top counterfeiters in the country. You don't get to the top of anything by being neurotic."

Lyons drove to the corner, turned and pulled the Blazer against the curb. "Anybody see any activity at the windows?"

Both Schwarz and Blancanales shook their heads. "It's weird," Gadgets said.

Lyons nodded. "The place has too many people inside to be quiet. If they were silence-sworn monks... maybe. But outlaw bikers? No way."

"So they know we're coming," Pol stated.

"I'd say that by now every hard-ass in the Black Hills knows we're coming," Schwarz replied. "We can thank old Nate Jenkins for that."

Lyons agreed again. "That means they're either getting ready to pull out—"

"Or ready to fight," Blancanales cut in. "Whichever way, there's no time like the present. Want me to take the front?"

The big ex-cop nodded. "Take Gadgets with you. Walk back slowly and give me time to get around back." He pulled the headset from his pocket and slipped it over his ears. "I'll tap you when I'm in position. Just like Cody—keep the Calicos covered until you hit the porch."

Gadgets and Pol both slipped their raincoats over their shoulders, exited the vehicle and started back down the block.

Lyons drove to the alley and turned in. There would be no element of surprise this time. The Able Team leader hit the accelerator, racing over the ground past picket fences and trash cans. He had no trouble identifying the backyard of the house in the middle of the block.

At least half a dozen more motorcycles were parked near the back door.

"You guys ready?" Lyons said into the mike in front of his face.

Two affirmatives came back.

"Then let's do it!" Lyons twisted the wheel hard, guiding the Blazer through the low picket fence in an explosion of crunching wood. Just inside the yard, he hit the brakes, skidding to a halt ten feet from the back door.

The Able Team leader dived from the vehicle, dragging the Calico behind him. He saw a bearded face appear in the window of the back door, then a rifle barrel shattered the glass, and a volley of automatic fire dug into the grass at his feet.

Lyons heard more gunfire from the front as he hit the ground on his shoulder, rolled forward and came to rest with his back against the house next to the door. Jamming the Calico around the frame, he angled the short barrel up and cut loose with his own burst of autofire.

Six 9 mm hollowpoints ripped through the aged wood in the back door. Lyons heard a stifled grunt, then a three-hundred-pound bearded biker fell through the splintered wood and onto his face in the yard. An AK-47 bounced past him.

The Able Team leader bounded to his feet as a second man, tall and slim and carrying an Uzi in one hand, burst out the back. In the other hand, the man carried a plastic case.

Lyons stayed against the wall, cutting loose with another half dozen 9 mm rounds that stitched up and down the biker's leathers and sent him crashing on top of his fat friend. The plastic case hit the ground and snapped the fasteners. A portable laser printer skidded across the grass.

Gunfire from the front—from an assortment of weapons, including the telltale Calicos—continued. Rising to his feet, Lyons laid down a two-second blanket of cover fire. Then, diving through the opening, he found himself in a deserted hallway.

It had to be the only empty area in the building, Lyons surmised. If the motorcycles and vans outside were any indication, there had to be at least two dozen men in the old two-story house.

The Calico held in assault mode in front of him, Lyons moved cautiously down the hall toward the first door on his right. It stood partially open, and from the angle at which he stood, he could see the corner of what appeared to be a chest of drawers.

Lyons crept cautiously toward the opening. He was two feet away when the stubby barrel of a gun poked out through the crack into the hallway.

The big ex-cop stepped to one side, firing from the hip. A stream of 9 mm bullets burped from the Calico as the machine pistol's light recoil tapped against his belly. The rounds blasted through the hollow-core door, which swung open to reveal a bald man wearing black leather chaps and a Harley T-shirt.

The biker held a massive .44 Magnum Colt Anaconda in his right hand. Blood poured from his multiple body wounds as he stared down at the holes in disbelief.

The Able Team leader tapped the trigger again and another burst of rounds stitched their way across the bald man's T-shirt. The big stainless-steel revolver fell to the hardwood floor.

The bald man tumbled on top of it.

Lyons moved swiftly now, dropping to a crouch as he swung the Calico into the bedroom. A man with a fuzzy goatee had moved back against the far wall, an M-14 service rifle gripped in shaking hands.

Lyons squeezed the trigger and another burst of hollowpoints flew into the man's denim vest and goatee. Dead hands closed around the .308 rifle as the biker slumped behind the bed.

Turning sideways, Lyons kept one eye on the hall door as he moved swiftly to the closet. Empty. He slid silently back across the ragged carpet to the hall.

A doorless entryway stood three feet away on the other side of the narrow corridor. Lyons leveled the Calico as he moved forward. As he advanced, he saw the kitchen. Vinyl-topped counters circled the room, with a matching island counter in the center.

The kitchen looked empty.

A head wearing a blue bandanna, tied pirate-style around the forehead, suddenly rose from behind the vinyl island. A shirtless, barbell-pumped torso followed. Attached to the sturdy trunk were twenty-inch arms that made the AK-47 they held look like a toy.

A burst of rifle rounds suddenly blasted toward Lyons, who dropped to one knee. The bullets sailed over his head as the Calico drilled 9 mm rounds back into the kitchen. The ex-cop's first three bullets struck the brawny chest, drawing tiny red dots in the well-defined pectoral area.

The bodybuilder opened his mouth in shock. Bright crimson blood poured out. It took another trio of rounds to take him down.

Lyons stepped into the kitchen, sweeping the room for more of the enemy. Sporadic gunfire still sounded from the front of the house.

An overweight biker and a frail man in leather, both toting pistols, suddenly appeared in the doorway to what Lyons assumed to be the living room. They cut near-comical figures as they tried to squeeze through the opening into the kitchen at the same time, getting momentarily stuck in a fashion reminiscent of Laurel and Hardy.

But the humor in Lyons's heart was short-lived as the two men spotted him, then retreated long enough to raise their weapons.

The ex-LAPD detective cut a figure eight back and forth between the two. A Glock 17 and a CZ-75 clattered to the kitchen tile. Laurel went down first. Hardy followed a second later, his huge body falling on top and causing the thinner man to nearly disappear.

Suddenly the house went silent.

The Able Team leader dropped below the counter once more, squeezing the Calico's twin magazine latches at the rear of the receiver and removing the partially spent drum. He held it under his armpit as he jerked the longer 100-round mag from the sling caddie, fit the bulkhead pin into the socket and snapped it into place.

Lyons shoved the 50-round drum into the off-side carrier as he rose again and made his way toward the living room. He dropped to one knee at the door and peered through.

Schwarz caught the movement and swung his weapon toward the kitchen. Lyons saw the knuckles on the electronics specialist's hand turn white then relax as he recognized his teammate.

Lyons stood and stepped into the room, letting his eyes ask the question as to Blancanales's whereabouts.

Schwarz answered with his own eyes, glancing at the ceiling, and Pol himself confirmed the answer as the first burst of gunfire suddenly exploded from the second story of the old Victorian house.

Lyons looked out of the living room to the front bedroom across the hall. "You've cleared it?" he whispered.

Schwarz nodded. "Pol took it, then went upstairs. I got pinned down in here." He indicated half a dozen biker bodies littering the furniture around the living room.

"Then let's go help him," Lyons said, turning toward the door. The Able Team warriors started up the stairs.

The firing picked up on the left side of the house. As he mounted the landing, Lyons saw a leather-clad body come flying through the door. He raised the Calico. To his side, Schwarz did the same.

Both Stony Man men lowered their weapons again as they saw the uselessness of their actions. The man was dead on his feet, riddled with 9 mm rounds that had to have come from Blancanales's Calico.

Lyons looked down the hall as a biker with a dirty blond ponytail dived from a doorway at the rear of the house. Schwarz turned and fired a steady stream of hollowpoints that hit the man and punched him to the floor.

The ex-cop studied the wall. Both doors evidently led to one long room that ran the length of the house. Otherwise, Pol wouldn't have been able to take out both of the last two men.

Lyons turned to Schwarz, nodding silently toward the other side of the hall. The electronics man nodded back, and moved out.

The Able Team leader hurried down the hall, stepping over the ponytailed corpse. As sporadic gunfire continued inside the long room, he took a deep breath and peered around the corner.

The room had been built to be a library. The first thing to catch Lyons's eye were the bookshelves that ran the length of both walls. But Cary Gamble and his pack of biker bodyguards weren't big readers, and the shelves were now covered with greasy scatterings of motorcycle and weapons parts.

Four men, clad in leather and denim, had taken refuge behind the couches and chairs around the room. Their backs to Lyons, they fired toward the front of the room at an overturned desk.

As Lyons watched, the hexagonal drum of a Calico appeared over the desktop and a burst of fire issued forth in his direction.

With another deep breath, Lyons flipped the selector switch on his weapon to semiauto. Unseen by the men in the room, he leaned in through the doorway. Looking through the rear peep site atop the 100-round drum, he let the white dot on the front post fall between the shoulder blades of a man wearing a denim vest and firing a Taurus PT-908.

As his finger moved back on the trigger, Lyons heard gunfire start on the other side of the hallway. Then a lone round drilled through the back of the man's vest and into his heart.

The other three men turned in unison as the Able Team leader flipped the selector back to full-auto. Holding the trigger back against the pistol grip, Lyons sent a 4-round explosion into the guts of a tall biker who squatted behind an armchair. Swinging the Calico to his left, he kept the trigger back. A stream of fire moved to a man who was attempting to maneuver his M-14 toward the rear assault. More of the Able Team leader's 9 mm Silvertips ripped through the man's belly, chest and neck.

As Lyons turned the Calico toward the final man in the room, he saw Pol rise from behind the desk. Blancanales's own 9 mm machine pistol sputtered in his hands, sending a full-auto stream of the bullets slicing their way through the body of a biker wearing a black cowboy hat.

For the second time in two minutes, the house fell silent.

Lyons's ears rang with the noise of gunfire as he motioned for Blancanales to follow him out of the room. The Able Team warriors made their way cautiously across the hall to the front bedroom, and saw a trio of outlaw bikers lying in pools of their own blood. A quick check of the closet and adjoining bath turned up nothing but an assortment of soiled leathers and denim.

The big ex-cop led the way back into the hall, past the stairs, to the final room at the rear of the house. He saw Schwarz standing in the middle of the room as he neared the door.

The rear upstairs bedroom had been converted to the printing room, but the counterfeiting equipment Lyons saw scattered around the room was different than what they'd found in Cody. Cary Gamble was of the new breed of counterfeiters, and the bullet-ridden computers and laser printers that now lay half-packed around the room were proof.

Schwarz held up a fistful of counterfeit bills and turned toward the door as the other two Able men entered. "Gentlemen," he said, "I'd like to introduce Mr. Cary Gamble." He pointed toward the body of a bearded man on the floor.

The man lay open-eyed, staring at the ceiling. A custom-worked full-house Government Model .45 was still gripped in his dead fingers. Red blood and lines of gray streaked the brown beard that covered his face, and more blood seeped from the khaki safari jacket worn over blue jeans. An old sweat-stained felt cowboy hat lay on the floor next to the corpse.

Lyons moved to an open suitcase full of hundred-dollar bills at Schwarz's feet, closed the clasps and lifted it.

Without another word, Able Team walked down the stairs and out of the house.

Stony Man Farm

AARON KURTZMAN RUBBED his bloodshot eyes, then lifted the telephone receiver to his ear. He held it between his head and shoulders as he found the intercom button for Barbara Price.

"Yeah, Bear?"

"I've got it, and yeah, there's a pattern. Why don't you come on in?" He heard the line click as Price hung up.

A few moments later, Kurtzman felt Price's hand on his shoulder.

"Okay," he said. "Take a look." He tapped the keyboard, opening seven windows on the screen. "Masters, Dvorek, O'Leary.... I've checked seven more of the men and women listed as killed during the Monaco strike five years ago. Every last one of them was either a cop or a career soldier from their respective countries. All of the cops resigned because of some problem like brutality or corruption. Most of the soldiers were dishonorably discharged, although one or two pulled a general."

"So we're talking about trained warriors who suddenly found themselves without a job."

"Precisely," Kurtzman said. "So, where do people like that usually go to put meat on the table?"

"The private sector. Mercenary or security work."

"The lady wins a cigar." Tapping the keys again, he opened subwindows beneath each victim. Names such as Johnson Safety and Security and Miami Mobile Patrol showed up under the English-speaking victims. Those from other countries bore foreign company names Kurtzman knew Price wouldn't be able to translate. But he also knew she'd figure it out from context.

Behind him, Kurtzman heard her draw in a deep breath. "You mean they all left the police or military and went into private security work?"

"Or a related field. Alarm systems, safety products, the like," Kurtzman replied. "Like you said, that isn't unusual for ex-cops or military. But all of them? I mean, you'd have thought at least one of them would have had a brother-in-law who'd have set them up in a fast-food restaurant or something, right?" He turned to face Price. "Okay, by itself, it's not much. But add it to the questionable conditions under which they left their other careers, and particularly the fact that they're still walking around five years after they were murdered, and I'd say there's more here than meets the eye."

"You're sure they're all still alive?" Price asked.

"No, but I'm making an educated guess that at least some of them are." His finger ran the keyboard, clearing the screen. A moment later the left side lighted up with the name William David Masters.

Masters had been a Temple, Texas, police officer who resigned when his finger had been caught in the till of a burglarized drugstore. He'd gone to work for Texas Investigation Consultants shortly thereafter. Masters stood six-one, weighed an even two hundred pounds, had a ruddy complexion with red hair and freckles, and his distinguishing marks consisted of a jagged facial scar that had come from a broken bottle during a rookie attempt to break up a bar fight.

Kurtzman pressed several more keys, and the other side of the screen took shape. It consisted of the physical description of a Huntsman Bolan had tracked down in England—6'1", 200 lbs, red hair, freckles and an irregular scar on left cheek that appeared to be the result of broken glass.

Kurtzman clasped his hands behind the back of his neck. "Descriptions of the other six I just checked matched up similarly, Barb. I'm about to compare the prints. If these aren't the same people, we've got one hell of a mathematical coincidence."

France

"So, AS I WAS SAYING, big guy," Jack Grimaldi said as he guided the plane's descent through the sky over the southern coast of France, "the Phoenicians founded a trading post here around 700 B.C. But the Genvoese built the castle in 1215."

Bolan shifted the satchel in his lap and looked down through the window to the natural harbor along the French Riviera. "Glad to see you've been doing your history homework, Jack," he said. "But I'm interested in Monaco's more recent past. Say, five years ago when the casino was hit. There's something dirty in this deal."

Grimaldi nodded as the wheels hit the runway. "Got to be. People who've been dead for five years rarely rise from the grave, start calling themselves the Huntsman and go around the world trying to assassinate folks. Fact is, I can't remember the last time it happened." His voice turned serious. "What do you think, Sarge? Terrorist sympathizers who faked their own deaths?"

Bolan shrugged as they taxied along the runway. "Maybe, but I don't think so. Aaron's got Akira and Hunt running further background investigations. But the ones they've already done didn't turn up any links. Not even any indications that they leaned toward radicalism."

Grimaldi pulled the plane to a halt and let the engine idle. "I don't understand it. They were positively IDed?"

"Yes and no." Bolan gathered his bags from the seat behind him and turned back to the pilot. "The casino burned, Jack. Some of the hostages with it. The people who seem to be turning up alive had to be identified through dental records. That leaves some room to play." Through the windshield, he saw a uniformed man exit a small glass building and head toward them.

The Executioner opened the door and started to step down.

Grimaldi reached out and grabbed his arm. "One other thing, Sarge."

One foot on the ground, Bolan turned back to the pilot.

Beneath his suede Alaskan bush pilot's cap, Grimaldi's eyebrows rose over his sunglasses. "The principality of Monaco officially passed to the Genvoese Grimaldi family in 1297. Got that? Grimaldi. You find some extra time on your hands while you're here, see if I might be on the shortlist for king or something."

Bolan chuckled as he pulled down his luggage. "You going to have a job for me?"

"You better believe it, big guy," Grimaldi said. "Chief Executioner."

The warrior slammed the door.

The uniformed man had arrived by the time Bolan turned around. A thin, neatly manicured pencil mustache lined his upper lip. Bowing stiffly, he said, "Mr. Michael Belasko?"

Bolan nodded.

"I am Captain Marc Grevin. Your Justice Department has arranged a meeting with the prefect of police in one hour." Turning on his heel, he led the way toward a dark sedan parked by the glass building. "I will escort you."

A moment later, the police officer opened the passenger's door for Bolan, circled the vehicle and slid behind the wheel. They cruised across the runway.

Bolan leaned back against the seat as they left the airport and entered La Condamine, one of the four districts of the tiny country. His tired eyes closed briefly as they passed through a residential resort area, and when they opened a few seconds later he saw several light-industrial buildings.

The Executioner didn't know where Monaco's police headquarters was located, but wherever it was, it wouldn't take an hour to get there. The entire country of Monaco covered less than one square mile.

Turning toward the driver, Bolan said, "We've got some time. Let's stop by the casino. I want to see where the attack went down."

The captain nodded. "Yes, if you like. But you remember that it was partially burned by the terrorists. It is highly unlikely that you will find any evidence that has not been found before."

Bolan shrugged and looked at his watch. "We've got an hour to kill. I just want to get a feel for the place." He settled back into his seat and closed his eyes again.

The Executioner had another reason for wanting to visit the casino, one he doubted Captain Grevin would understand. Bolan had fought the injustices of the world for more years than he cared to remember.

Those battles had taken him down unknown roads the world over. And during his long hard war, the Executioner had developed what some people called a sixth sense. Something was pulling Mack Bolan toward the casino.

Grevin took the next corner and they entered Monte Carlo. A few seconds later, he pulled into a yellow No Parking zone in front of the casino. Bolan looked up the steps to see the concrete face of the building.

The Executioner hadn't been in the casino since the fire five years earlier, but he couldn't help thinking that it had been rebuilt hurriedly. Concrete, plastic and other modern building materials had taken the place of the ornately carved wood he remembered. But more than the wood had been lost to the fire. Much of the atmosphere that had made the casino famous had gone up in flames, as well.

Grevin engaged the emergency brake and started to open the door.

Bolan shook his head. "I'd rather go in alone, Captain. I don't know if there's still a connection to this place, but it might be better if I'm not seen with you."

Grevin nodded. "I understand."

The warrior exited the vehicle and fell in with a Japanese tour group as they mounted the steps to the casino. He was greeted in the lobby by a man wearing a smartly pressed black tuxedo, then entered the main gambling room.

He moved to the line in front of the chip window and took a place behind a tall dark-haired man in a gray pin-striped suit. As he waited, the Executioner's trained eyes combed the gambling apparatuses before him. Every game of chance known to man seemed to be in the room, and every culture on earth appeared to be represented. Business suits and formal gowns mingled with more casually dressed men and women in slacks and even jeans.

The man in the gray suit in front of him finished at the window, and Bolan stepped up to trade five hundred dollars for the brightly colored chips. He moved toward the oblong roulette table and saw the man in the gray suit stop at the bar along the wall. The bartender turned, pulled a bottle of Southern Comfort off a shelf and poured the man a shot.

Squeezing in at the roulette table between a woman in a navy blue sequinned gown and a man in a Western suit and cowboy boots, Bolan took a place near the wheel in the center of the felt-covered table.

The warrior dropped a fifty-dollar chip on red as he continued to scan the room. It was a world-renowned casino, but the Executioner saw nothing remarkable to tell him why the terrorists had chosen to attack here five years ago. Nor was there any indication of a connection to the people who had supposedly died in the flames.

The wheel spun and the steel ball bounced three times before falling into the black compartment marked 32. Bolan watched the rake pull his chip away.

He dropped two more of the markers on red, and glanced up to see the man who had stood in front of him at the chip window move up to the table across from him. Gray suit took a sip of his drink, then dropped several chips on the green felt and stared at the wheel.

The wheel spun again, the ball dropping this time on 4. Gray Suit muttered something under his breath as his chips disappeared. He pulled several more from his pocket, scattering them at strategic points across the layout.

Bolan watched the rake push chips his way this time. He let them ride, then lost again when the ball came to rest next on 19.

Gray Suit moved to the end of the table in an apparent effort to change his luck. Bolan moved his bet to black, but found his eyes stayed on the dark-complected man with the black hair.

There was something about him, something familiar. The Executioner had either met the man sometime in the past, or he bore a striking resemblance to someone Bolan knew.

The wheel spun again, then again. The warrior and Gray Suit continued to place their bets, winning some of the spins, losing others. The Executioner didn't know what the man was up to, but of one thing he was certain: the guy was making his way closer to where Bolan stood.

The warrior's hand moved inconspicuously to his belt buckle. From there, he could sweep back the tail of his unbuttoned jacket and have the Desert Eagle in hand in a heartbeat.

Gray Suit moved in silently next to Bolan and dropped his final three chips on the table in front of him. The distinct scent of Southern Comfort wafted up into the Executioner's nostrils as the man moved all three chips over the 16.

The wheel spun, then the ball finally dropped on 24. A mixture of curses and utterances of glee came from around the table.

The warrior watched out of the corner of his eye. Gray Suit muttered under his breath, then reached for the pile of chips that had been in front of him. Realizing he had bet them all, he casually slipped his hand inside his suit coat.

Bolan's battle radar went to red. The man's movement was a little too smooth, a little too practiced.

The Executioner's hand dropped to the butt of the Desert Eagle.

At the same time, Bolan saw a clear plastic hypodermic needle appear in the man's hand. The big .44 was halfway out of the holster when the Executioner felt someone slam into his side.

Bolan struck the edge of the table as the hypo shot forward over his shoulder. His gun hand was shoved under the table. He twisted, facing up in time to see the scowl on Gray Suit's face.

The needle held in an ice-pick grip, his thumb on the plunger, the man raised it over his head to try again.

Bolan cleared the Desert Eagle of leather and tried to raise it. The barrel of the big .44 struck the underside of the roulette table with a thud.

Gray Suit's arm began to descend.

As he brought his left arm up to block, Bolan felt a pair of hands grasp his elbow and wrist, halting the movement.

The Executioner jerked violently to one side as the needle came down, at the same time twisting his wrist beneath the table and pulling the trigger of the Desert Eagle. The explosion sounded like an atomic bomb within the casino, and a hush fell over the room.

Gray Suit roared in pain as the .44 Magnum hollowpoint round drilled through his pant leg, scorching the skin of his calf. The hypodermic needle missed the Executioner's arm by a hairbreadth, snagging in the arm of his sport coat. He twisted back the other way, and his attacker lost his grip on the needle.

The warrior fired again, another magnum round drilling into the floor. The new explosion helped the crowd within the casino find their voices. Screams and shrieks replaced the silence.

The scowl on Gray Suit's face turned to a crazed expression of rage. He backpedaled from the roulette table and disappeared behind a group of horrified onlookers.

Bolan felt the hand on his elbow give way as he twisted again, bringing the Desert Eagle up from under the table. He turned toward the hand still grasping his wrist in time to see a stocky man in his late forties reach inside his own jacket.

The warrior caught his balance on the table, using his free hand to shove off as the man stepped back and a SIG-Sauer P-226 came into view.

"The Huntsman cannot die!" the man yelled. "The Wild Hunt continues." He shoved the barrel of the 9 mm pistol into his mouth.

Bolan lunged forward.

His hand grasped the P-226 just as the Huntsman pulled the trigger.

The Executioner dropped his hand in disgust and let the man fall to the floor. Turning, he sprinted toward the front door, shouldering screaming bystanders out of the way. On the front steps, he scanned the parking lot.

The man in the gray suit wasn't hard to find. Down the steps and a good forty yards away, he stood next to Captain Grevin's sedan. His face livid with rage, he shouted through the open window at the police officer.

Bolan raised the Desert Eagle, aligning the sights on the man's head. As his finger moved back on the trigger, he saw his target draw a long-barreled automatic pistol and jam it through the car window.

The second unexpected jolt in two minutes knocked the Executioner's hand to one side. The .44 Magnum round went wild as the Desert Eagle exploded.

At the same time, Bolan heard a soft cough from the area of Captain Grevin's car.

Turning to the right, the Executioner saw a tiny frightened security guard aiming a Walther PPK at his face.

Bolan turned back to the parking lot.

The dark man in the gray suit had disappeared again.

6

Israel

Gary Manning knelt in the van, unfolding a wheelchair Phoenix Force had just picked up at Bethlehem Medical Supply. David McCarter stood hunched over in the van, trying valiantly to adjust the length of the crutches that had come from the same store while Calvin James, his brown eyes hidden behind black sunglasses, tapped the white tip of his new cane on the floor.

"So," Encizo said, looking up from his seat on the floor of the van, "you figure the guy in the corduroy cap is their sentry?" The little Cuban wore the white slacks and pullover top of a medical attendant.

Katz shrugged. "It's impossible to be sure. But even if he isn't a lookout, they might have another one. In any case, the administrator who found me in the back hall is in league with them—of that I'm certain." He turned to Manning, who had the chair unfolded. "You and Rafael go first," he said. "Rafe, wheel him to the side of the hall and get one of the blue forms from the pad at the reception counter."

Encizo nodded. "What if they ask me something, Katz? My Hebrew isn't much better than my Martian."

Katz smiled. "It used to be called deaf and dumb. Now I believe it is referred to as mute and hearing impaired. But regardless of what you call this disability, it seems that this would be the perfect time for you to acquire it."

Encizo chuckled. He opened the door, glanced around, then exited and pulled the wheelchair after him.

Manning held a lumpy blanket as he climbed down, took a seat and spread the covering across his knees. Encizo wheeled his patient down the sidewalk, then disappeared around the corner.

"Give them five minutes, David," Katz told McCarter. "You're next."

"Bully," the Briton said. He turned to James. "Perhaps Ray Charles here will entertain us with a quick rendition of 'Hit the Road, Jack' while we wait."

James grinned behind the sunglasses. "I lean more toward Stevie Wonder," he said. "How about 'Ebony and Ivory'? You can sing the Paul McCartney part."

McCarter glanced at his watch, then stood. "Maybe later. Right now, I'm afraid it's time for me to limp off into the sunset." The van door slid open again and he was gone.

"You don't think there's going to be a problem with the black skin here in Israel?" James asked Katz, lifting the sunglasses off his face for a moment.

"There are more black Jews than you realize," the Israeli stated.

He waved a hand at the door. "Go."

As soon as James had disappeared around the corner, Katz glanced at his watch. He would give it two more minutes, then return to the Evaluation Center himself to lead the attack downstairs.

Katz readied himself, lifted the duffel bag, drew the drawstring and stepped out of the van. He felt his heart race as it always did before impending battle, and quickened his pace.

The Israeli turned the corner and saw the Evaluation Center ahead. He hurried on, the knot in his stomach pushing his feet forward. As he turned up the sidewalk to the front entrance, he saw Manning in the wheelchair against the wall. Encizo stood behind him.

McCarter had taken a seat on one of the metal chairs, propping the crutches against the wall as he worked on the blue form in his lap with a ballpoint pen.

Calvin James, complete with cane and dark glasses, had just tapped his way to the window and was ripping a blue form off the pad.

The man in the corduroy cap sat in the same chair he had before. His eyes flitted from James to McCarter to Encizo, the expression on his face that of a man trying to make an important decision. He glanced out the front door and saw Katz.

The expression on his face suddenly changed as the decision was finally made.

Katz's pace quickened again as the man in the corduroy cap pulled the walkie-talkie from inside his coat. The radio went to his lips.

The ruse was over. The man *was* a sentry, and he had put two and two together and come up with four.

The Phoenix Force leader reached into the duffel bag and drew the sound-suppressed mini-Uzi. He broke into a sprint as he shrugged into the weapon's sling.

The man in the cap saw the gun and jerked a CZ-75 from somewhere inside his clothes. Standing, he trained the barrel on James's back.

"Calvin!" Katz shouted as he lifted the subgun.

James turned toward the sound, as did Manning, McCarter, Encizo and the rest of the men and women waiting in the hall.

Katz dropped the Uzi's sights on the man with the Czech 9 mm. His finger moved back on the trigger, sending a muffled 3-round burst into the Bloody Wind sentry. But even as he fired, Yakov Katzenelenbogen felt his heart sink.

He had been a split second too late. A lone 9 mm round from the CZ-75 had preceded his burst.

The Phoenix Force leader saw Calvin James slump to the floor, the white-tipped cane clattering across the tile and rolling to a rest against the cold concrete wall.

Omaha, Nebraska

"DR. MCALMON WILL BE with you as soon as he finishes with his patient," the receptionist said as she ushered Carl Lyons into a waiting room. "If you'd like to have a seat, Agent Johnson..." She let her voice trail off as she closed the door behind her.

Lyons dropped onto an overstuffed couch against the wall. Across the room stood several toy shelves. Trucks, dolls and building blocks were carefully stacked. On the wall above the shelves was a framed poster of "Tommy Tooth." The giant cartoon molar with arms and legs was admonishing a group of children to floss as well as brush.

The Able Team leader's eyes dropped to the stack of magazines on the end table next to him. He lifted a *Sports Illustrated* magazine and turned to an article on Dennis Byrd, the New York Jets defensive lineman who'd broken his neck during a game a few years earlier. The picture showed Byrd—whom doctors had predicted would be paralyzed for life—on an exercise bike.

The ex-cop's mind started the story, then drifted away. Stony Man had pulled Able Team off the counterfeit detail as soon as the information about the casino victims being identified by dental records had fallen into place. Using their Justice Department credentials provided by Brognola, he, Schwarz and Blancanales had been double-checking the dental records of the people Schwarz now called the "living dead."

Lyons had been to two clinics already. Both dentists had confirmed their earlier identifications. Now he was waiting to check the records of one David Richard Rickman, a former employee of Randolph Security.

The Able Team leader dropped the magazine to his lap. What it all boiled down to was simple: according to the existing dental records, the people who had been in the Monaco casino fire were dead.

Simple?

Not really. According to the same people's fingerprints, they were now running around the world killing people.

The door opened and a big man with black plastic-rimmed glasses and salt-and-pepper hair entered the room carrying a manila file. He stopped in the middle of the room and pulled a pair of transparent rubber gloves from his hands as he said, "Special Agent Johnson?"

Lyons nodded as he dropped the magazine back in the rack and stood up. "Dr. McAlmon," he said, reaching out to shake the man's extended hand. "I won't take up much of your time."

McAlmon waved a hand in front of his face. "Take as much of it as you need. I've got a son in the FBI. Always glad to help." He turned, dropped the gloves into a trash can behind him, then faced Lyons. "Marge says this is about the Rickman deal? I brought the file, but there's no need for me to look at it. I remember the case well."

"What makes you remember it?" Lyons wondered.

McAlmon shrugged. "I've identified several bodies over the years, but this was the only one outside the United States. Besides that, Mr. Rickman was in for a checkup shortly before leaving on the trip. He was excited about having won it. In fact, that was about all we talked abou—"

Lyons felt a light bulb suddenly flicker in his brain. "You say he *won* the trip to Monaco?" he interrupted.

"Yes, that's what he said. Some kind of company raffle contest or something, if I remember that part correctly."

"Doctor," Lyons said, "I'm not at liberty to disclose the details, but there are things about this case that just flat don't make any sense. Is there any chance of a mistake?"

McAlmon shook his head. "No, Agent Johnson, I don't think so. I double- and triple-checked my comparison. I'd hate to make a mistake on a situation of this importance...not to mention that the Randolph account makes up a decent percentage of my business."

The light bulb flickered brighter. "You do a lot of business with their company?" he asked.

McAlmon nodded. "At least half of it, I imagine. They carry the dental policies through an HMO. There are only three dentists on the list, and one of them drinks so heavily his practice is about gone."

"Then you've got their employees coming and going through these offices all the time?"

McAlmon shrugged. "Two of them are waiting down the hall right now," he said, frowning. "I'm not sure what you're getting at, Agent Johnson."

Lyons held out his hand. "I'm not sure myself. But I'll find out. Thank you for your help, Dr. McAlmon."

The tall man shook his hand. "Anytime."

The big ex-cop showed himself out through a side door and walked to the Blazer parked in the lot. He glanced at his watch as he slid behind the wheel. Schwarz and Blancanales were off checking other dentists. He had twenty minutes before he was to meet them at a café two blocks away.

Lyons settled back against the seat. Okay, what had he learned? First, Rickman had won the trip to Monaco through a company contest. Had the other victims won their trips, as well? If so, the contests sounded rigged.

But more importantly, it sounded as if someone wanted to make sure specific people were in the casino when it was attacked.

Lyons rubbed his eyes. Second, he hadn't known that Dr. McAlmon did at least half of Randolph Security's dental work, and that in itself presented some interesting possibilities. It meant that if Randolph, or someone connected to the company, was behind this whole thing, they could not only have manipulated the contest so that specific people won the trips, they could run someone in as a dental patient who might have the opportunity to switch dental records.

He opened his eyes with a start. The sudden realization that he was thinking too small hit him like a brick between the eyes.

All of the casino victims had been ex-cops or soldiers who worked for security firms. Stony Man already knew that. But what if all of the rent-a-cop businesses were tied into each other somehow? Maybe owned by the same giant umbrella company? If all of the employees carried dental plans for their employees, every one of them could have sponsored a bogus trip contest, and chosen who they wanted in the casino that night.

And switched that person's dental records with those of the poor bastards whose bodies were found in the fire.

Lyons let air blow through his teeth as the enormity of the plan hit him again. The former LAPD detective didn't know exactly how the pieces of the puzzle fit together yet.

But he knew the pieces were there.

Reaching under the dashboard, the Able Team leader lifted the microphone to his lips. "Able One to Stony Man."

Barbara Price's voice came back immediately. "Go ahead, Ironman."

"Barb, get Bear or one of his bunch to check and see if all of the security companies carried their people's dental policies on an HMO plan with limited dentists to choose from."

"Got it, Able One," Price said. "Anything else?"

"Affirmative." He told Price about the contest Rickman had won, and requested that the computer crew check to see if the other victims had been "lucky winners," as well. "Then somebody needs to start running down any connection there might be between the different companies," he said. "You might—"

Lyons stopped speaking as the Blazer's windshield suddenly exploded into a shower of glass. As he dropped the microphone and ducked under the dashboard, bursts of automatic rifle fire saturated the vehicle from all sides.

Monaco

THE OFFICE OF MONACO'S prefect of police was a prototype for self-idolization.

The wall behind the desk was covered with pictures of the prefect, Paul LaSalle, shaking hands with what appeared to be every dignitary and celebrity born in the twentieth century. Representing the United States, Presidents Ford, Carter, Reagan, and Bush smiled into the camera as they grasped the hand of Monaco's top cop. Below the presidents, Bolan saw Henry Kissinger, Norman Schwarzkopf and a host of other dignitaries.

The warrior watched the gray-haired man behind the desk speak softly into the phone, then turned to his right. That wall had been devoted to what appeared to be LaSalle's pursuit of every sport known to man. Bodybuilding: LaSalle flexed his biceps in a tank top in front of a Nautilus machine. Karate: the police chief, dressed in a stiffly pressed white gi, executed a side kick. Soccer: a much younger LaSalle raised his hands over his head in victory as the ball passed the opposing goalie and struck the net at the rear of the goal. Mixed in between were sailing, skiing, scuba diving and other pictures, and like the wall behind his desk, the photographs were blanketed so tightly that only tiny wisps of the green paint on the wall peeked occasionally through between the frames.

Finally LaSalle dropped the phone back into the cradle and looked up. His eyes were pained, his face slightly red. "I regret to inform you that Captain Greven passed away on the operating table ten minutes ago." He sighed, looking up at the ceiling. "I regret even more to admit that your suspicion appears to be correct."

Bolan nodded. Paul LaSalle was full of himself— the photographs proved that. But so far, he had been open and honest with the Executioner.

Something Bolan couldn't say for Captain Greven.

LaSalle shook his head. "I had one of my inspectors initiate an investigation the moment you told me this mysterious man in the gray suit had been shouting at Greven before he shot him. As you yourself indicated, it did not seem to be the thing a man attempting to flee would take the time to do."

The Executioner nodded again. "If Greven had tried to stop him, yeah, sure, I could see it. But he didn't. The captain was still sitting in the car. His weapon hadn't even been drawn. I got the distinct impression that the guy knew your captain."

This time it was LaSalle's turn to nod. He glanced at the phone, crossing his hands on the desk in front of him. "My inspector just informed me that during the past week one hundred and fifteen thousand francs have been deposited into two bank accounts bearing Greven's name." The man's jaw tightened. "Captain Greven set you up to be killed, Mr. Belasko," he said. "No matter how much I apologize, I cannot make up for that."

Bolan shrugged. "There are good cops and bad cops," he said. "And sometimes good cops who have a weak moment and go bad." He stared the man in the face. "Nobody's blaming you."

"And you were treated quite shabbily by casino security, I understand," LaSalle added.

Bolan repressed a chuckle, his mind returning to the frightened guard who had taken him into custody. The man's hands had shaken so badly that the Executioner had been more afraid he'd be shot by mistake than on purpose. "He couldn't have known what was going on," he said. "All he saw was a guy shooting a big gun and another guy in a gray suit trying to get away from him."

LaSalle looked relieved. Slowly the color began to fade from his face. "Is there any way I can make this up to you?"

The Executioner nodded. "Cooperation," he stated. "That'll make up for it in spades." He paused. "Have you heard anything from your forensic lab yet?"

LaSalle frowned. "No," he said, reaching for the phone again. "And they should be finished by now." He tapped in a number, then pressed a button on the console and set the receiver back in the cradle.

Bolan heard the line ring over the speakerphone. The call was answered in French on the second ring.

"This is LaSalle. Put me through to Onfroi."

A moment later, a high-pitched voice answered. "Onfroi."

LaSalle looked at Bolan. "Do you speak French?"

"Yeah. But my English is better."

"Speak in English, Georges," he said. "And tell us what you have found."

The unseen man on the other end cleared his throat. "It was a strong solution of potassium." Had the attack been successful, it would have appeared that Mr. Belasko had suffered a heart attack. His potassium level would have been above the normal range of 3.4 to 5.2 percent, but not so high as to have drawn undo notice." He cleared his throat again. "Are you listening, Mr. Belasko?"

"Yes."

"My guess is that your blood would have shot up to around nine percent potassium. Enough to kill you, but not enough to immediately suspect you had been poisoned. Will there be anything else?"

LaSalle looked at Bolan, who shook his head.

"No, Georges," the prefect said. "Thank you." He tapped another button and the line went dead. He turned back to Bolan. "What can I do to assist you now?"

Bolan hesitated. He had learned several valuable things since arriving in Monaco. First, there were police officers who could be bought. Second, there was a man working with whoever fronted the Huntsman who was not one of the assassins. This man didn't stick a gun in his mouth as soon as it looked like he might be caught, nor did he spout the strange mantra about the "Huntsman never dying."

No, the dark-haired man in the gray suit hadn't been a robotlike Huntsman. Yet there had been something about the man's mannerisms that reminded Bolan of the Huntsman. And the Executioner would have bet his bottom dollar that if he had searched the man's pockets, he'd have found a Vietnamese beer bottle cap somewhere.

And third, even though he was not a Huntsman, this man operated very much like they did. He was a stone-cold killer, and he was good enough to come close to doing what hundreds of trained assassins had tried and failed to get done over the years.

Kill the Executioner.

Somewhere within the huge puzzle that seemed to get more complicated with each additional piece, these three new facts played a vital part. Bolan didn't know where they fit, but if anyone could figure it out, he knew who that man was.

"Mr. Belasko?" LaSalle prompted, frowning at the Executioner.

Bolan looked up, realizing he had been lost for a moment in thought.

"I repeat," LaSalle said. "What else can I do to assist you?"

The warrior stood. "Do you have a secure phone line in here?"

LaSalle smiled. "Why, of course."

The Executioner didn't expect what he said next to come out sounding quite so harsh. "Then get out and let me use it."

LaSalle appeared to take no offense.

A moment later, Monaco's prefect of police was shutting his office door behind him.

Mack Bolan dialed Stony Man Farm.

Israel

THE SOUND-SUPPRESSED mini-Uzi clutched in assault mode, Katz sprinted through the doorway of the Evaluation Center amid the screams of the disabled men and women in the chairs against the wall. As he crossed the threshold, he saw Encizo step from behind the wheelchair and swing his own machine pistol out from under the medical smock.

Manning rose from the chair, producing another of the suppressed mini-Uzis from under the blanket covering his legs. McCarter's crutches fell to the sides as his Browning Hi-Power came out of his jacket.

The man in the brown corduroy cap fell back into his chair, his body going limp as his eyes stared lifelessly into space.

The Phoenix Force leader let the Uzi fall to the end of the sling, snatched the Czech pistol from the man's hand and flipped the safety up. He shoved the CZ-75 into his waistband and turned to James.

The Phoenix Force warrior had slid to a sitting position against the wall, his hand clutching his abdomen. "Go on!" he yelled over the pandemonium from the people in the hallway. "It's just a flesh wound!"

Katz dropped to a knee at James's side, throwing the man's coat open and ripping the buttons off the bloody shirt. The bullet had caught James as he turned, scraping across the front of his belly. On many men, it would have done nothing more than rid them of an inch or so of unwanted fat.

But on James, there was no fat of which to be rid.

Katz studied the wound. It didn't look serious, but the abdomen was a "bloody" part of the body, and wounds could be deceiving. In any case, there was no time for an in-depth diagnosis, and he couldn't afford to take chances.

Looking up, Katz yelled, "Rafe!"

The little Cuban hurried over.

"Get him back to the van."

"No!" James protested as Encizo squatted and grabbed him under the arms. "I'm all right!"

Phoenix Force had worked together so long that it sometimes seemed as if they were all hooked into one central brain. Each of them was a leader in his own right, perfectly capable of taking control of the team whenever the situation dictated it.

Katz rarely had to pull rank, but he did so now.

"Go back to the van. Now!"

James nodded, letting Encizo help him to his feet.

Katz turned to the remaining two Phoenix Force warriors. "Let's go!" he said, then tucked the duffel bag under his arm and sprinted down the hall after the two men.

The Phoenix Force leader scowled as he ran. The odds had been stacked against them already, and now their force had been cut almost by half. An old battle adage claimed that wounding an enemy was better than killing him—a dead man decreased the enemy forces by only one, but an injured man required care, and took others away from the fight, as well.

That maxim had just been proved correct.

Had the man in the corduroy cap warned the Bloody Wind terrorists hidden in the basement below? Katz didn't know. But he had to assume the worst. In any case, the Israeli knew he would soon find out.

Manning reached the adjoining hall first, with McCarter at his heels. The big Canadian slid to a stop on the slick tile, his Uzi aimed ahead of him, waist-high. The Briton fell in behind him, his Hi-Power at the ready. Katz could see that the former SAS commando had threaded his own sound-suppressor onto the barrel of the Browning, and traded the normal 13-round magazine for a box of twenty that extended below the grip.

Katz slowed as he reached the two men. He dropped the duffel bag to the ground, pulled out his prosthesis and shrugged into the man-made limb. He watched Manning peer around the corner, then followed the Canadian and Briton into the hallway leading to the stairs.

The Phoenix Force leader finished tying the prosthesis into place half a second before the stairwell door flew open.

He grabbed his dangling subgun as two men dressed in T-shirts and olive-drab fatigue pants barreled through the door. The first man, his face pitted with the scars of adolescent acne, raised a Russian-made AKM with the stock folded as he stepped out into the hall. Just behind him, an older man clutching an M-1 Garand stopped in the doorway.

Manning held the trigger back on his Uzi, giving the acne-scarred terrorist a quick zip of quiet 9 mm parabellum rounds that stitched him belt to sternum. He fell forward, dropping the folded rifle.

The older man tried to bring the bulky Garand into play, but the barrel struck the door frame.

The microsecond's delay cost him his life.

McCarter fired a double tap from his Browning, catching the Bloody Wind terrorist in the heart and throat. The man toppled onto his comrade on the floor.

Katz slid between McCarter and Manning, taking the lead. He moved into the semilit stairwell, pressing his back against the cool concrete blocks. The stairs were deserted, but below, he could hear excited voices.

The Israeli descended the stairs, walking a fine line between speed and silence. Only two men had come up the stairs, which meant they had been sent to check out the report by the man in the corduroy cap.

The greater part of the element of surprise might be gone, but a shred remained.

Katz reached the bottom of the stairs, hearing the soft footsteps of McCarter and Manning come to a halt behind him. Directly ahead, he saw a hallway he had to assume followed the same path as the one directly above it. Across the hall stood a screen-enclosed room. Behind the screen, chairs, desks and filing cabinets had been stacked on top of one another. A wooden door frame had been built into the framing. A simple combination padlock secured the door.

Could any of the terrorists be hiding inside the storage area? Katz didn't know. The locked padlock couldn't have been reached through the screen, but it could have been secured by someone staying outside.

Katz moved to the screen, his eyes sweeping the area, the Uzi ready. He saw nothing suspicious.

Voices from the other end of the building forced him to turn away. He paused, drawing a deep breath. There was no assurance that the basement was a duplicate of the floor above. But the storage room lay directly beneath the vacant classrooms he had observed earlier on his recon mission.

Which meant that they were at the rear of the building. Whatever else did lay beneath the ground, lay behind them. The Stony Man warriors would just have to round the corners blindly and see what they found.

Katz turned, silently waving Manning to the left. He pointed to McCarter, tapped his own chest, then motioned right. With another deep breath, he started for the corner.

The hallway *did* follow the same plan as the floor above, and Katz moved quietly to the adjoining passageway. As he neared the corner, he heard footsteps running toward him. Pressing his back against the wall, he waited.

A sprinting man in green fatigues rounded the corner. A Government Model .45 was strapped to his waist in a flap holster.

Katz's foot shot out, tripping the man.

The man fumbled for the holstered weapon as he hit the floor. A soft *pfffft* echoed down the hall as McCarter drilled a lone 9 mm round through the terrorist's brain.

The Phoenix Force leader peered around the corner cautiously. The adjacent hall led toward the front of the building, but had only one door to the right. One room, then. A big one. Probably a conference room.

Through the opening, Katz caught a brief glimpse of green as a Bloody Wind gunner hurried past.

An open area lay behind the stairwell, and the Israeli presumed the hall down which Manning was now headed had to hold a similar room.

Cautiously he moved around the corner.

Katz kept his back to the wall as he slid past the stairwell. He saw Manning appear on the other side of the hall, nod toward the door ahead of him, then slide silently toward it. The Israeli moved to the opposite wall, his Uzi ready to fire as he catfooted to the opening.

Stopping at the edge of the door, Katz glanced over his shoulder. McCarter was right behind him. He looked across the open area to Manning. They would need to hit both rooms simultaneously.

The Phoenix Force leader held up his fist. His index finger shot up.

One.

Katz's middle finger followed.

Two.

The Stony Man warriors rounded their respective corners as Katz's ring finger joined the others.

The question as to what lay behind the door was answered as Katz's eyes swept the room. It had been built as a conference room, but the long folding table now rested on its side, leaning against the far wall, its legs doubled under it. Folding chairs, armchairs and even a few couches scattered the room, with three of the couches forming a "conversation pit" in front of a television in the corner to the right.

The heads of eight men suddenly jerked toward the doorway. All of them held weapons.

A steady burst of 5.45 mm rounds from the AK-SU in the hands of a terrorist wearing a red hooded sweatshirt kicked off the carnage.

Katz dropped to one knee beneath the assault. He held the trigger back on his minigun, catching the sweatshirt with half a dozen 9 mm rounds that sent the man sprawling to his back over a coffee table.

Out of the corner of his eye, Katz saw McCarter gripping the Browning in both hands. The muzzle rose and fell, then rose again, as the former SAS commando drove another Bloody Wind gunner back against the folded conference table. The table rocked against the wall, then crashed to the floor on top of the dead terrorist.

A mighty 12-gauge roar threatened to deafen Katz. He felt a hot rush of wind against his face. The blast sailed by, striking the wall and sending concrete dust floating through the air like a snowstorm.

The Phoenix Force leader swung his mini-Uzi toward the shotgunner as he pumped the slide of a Mossberg 500. The weapon flew from the man's hands as a burst of 9 mm slugs ripped through his torso.

To his side, Katz saw McCarter's Browning lock open, empty. Almost as quickly, the magazine fell to the floor. The Briton reached to his belt for another 20-rounder.

Another barrage of gunfire came from the enemy. One of the bullets struck the magazine in McCarter's hand and sent it flying through the air, forcing him to dive for cover behind a stuffed armchair.

Katz swept the CZ-75 from his waistband and tossed it toward the Briton. "David!" he yelled as it sailed through the air.

McCarter shoved the Browning into his belt, caught the CZ by the barrel with his left hand, and transferred it to his right all in one smooth motion. A second later, two more Bloody Wind gunners lay dead.

Bursts of gunfire from both sides sent Katz somersaulting forward to the concealment of a ragged brown couch. More rounds ripped through the material, ricocheting off the metal inside and making the springs sing above the gunfire.

Katz rolled onto his back, tight against the base of the couch. On the other side of the room, he could hear McCarter's return fire. Then, for a moment, the firing stopped.

The Phoenix Force leader felt the couch move slightly as someone climbed onto the front. His eyes stared upward.

Slowly a bearded face inched over the backrest of the couch. First came the top of the head, and Katz saw the man had dark curly hair. Next, came the hairline, and the Israeli could see that the man he was about to kill was going bald.

Katz waited until the eyes moved over the top of the couch, then blew them out of their sockets with a triple burst of 9 mm rounds.

More automatic gunfire riddled the couch. Rounds struck the front legs, and the frazzled piece of furniture tilted forward. Another round burned along Katz's arm, scorching his shirtsleeve.

The Israeli dropped the near-empty magazine from his weapon and shoved a fresh box up the grips. Rolling to his stomach, he darted away from the death trap on all fours, rising to a squatting position as soon as he was in sight.

A man wearing a faded denim vest above his fatigue pants stood firing across the room at the chair where McCarter had gone to ground. Katz dropped him with half a magazine of 9 mm semijacketed hollowpoints.

Only two enemy guns still fired. One of the men had taken refuge behind the conversation pit in front of the TV. The other fired from behind an upturned end table across the room.

"Please! Please!" begged the man behind the conversation pit. "I give up! Do not shoot me!"

The gunfire behind the coffee table stopped as the man spoke.

"Drop your weapon!" Katz ordered. "Raise your hands above your head and stand up. Slow."

A clank sounded behind the couches across the room. Two hands moved up into sight. The head came next, then the terrorist struggled from his knees to a standing position, his face a mask of horror.

"Traitor!" roared a voice from behind the coffee table. A long burst followed. The first rounds missed the surrendering terrorist, smashing into the wall behind him, more bullets striking the television screen and sending sparks and smoke flying from the appliance. The man behind the coffee table corrected his aim, and the last of the onslaught cut his comrade to shreds.

Katz swung his subgun toward the coffee table, but McCarter had already risen behind the chair, vaulted another of the couches and moved behind the avenging terrorist. He pumped three rounds from the CZ-75 into the man's back. The last terrorist fell forward, knocking the coffee table over and falling to his death on top of it.

The Phoenix Force leader sensed movement behind him and swung toward the door. Manning stood holding his Uzi down at his side. Trails of smoke drifted from the barrel.

The Israeli hurried to the door and stared at the big Canadian.

Manning shook his head.

Katz crossed the hall. The room opposite had been a conference room at one time, too. It had been cleared of all furniture, and bare striped mattresses and soiled blankets now covered the floor—along with the bodies of the six men who had lain atop them.

He stepped back into the hall, letting the Uzi fall to the end of the sling. With the other two Phoenix Force warriors at his heels, Katz started down the hall. He had reached the stairs when he caught a glimmer of movement in the storage area behind the screen.

He half turned as a hand appeared behind the wire holding a pistol. Above the gun, he saw a snarling face.

The Israeli knew he'd never get the Uzi into play in time. Raising his prosthesis, he pointed the plastic index finger toward the terrorist, flexed his pectoral muscle against the trigger mechanism and fired a .22 Magnum round.

A tiny red hole appeared in the forehead above the hate-filled eyes. The final Bloody Wind gunner fell against the screen, dead.

Katz turned, and they started up the steps.

7

Omaha, Nebraska

Carl Lyons had never been particularly fond of armoring street vehicles. In his opinion, the weight required to make an average sedan bulletproof slowed it to the point that the disadvantage outweighed the advantage. And no matter how hard you worked, there were still soft spots in whatever protective covering you chose to use.

Not to mention that most vehicle armor couldn't withstand explosives.

No, Lyons had always been of the opinion that, for most missions, it made more sense to rely on being well armed, staying alert to potential threats, utilizing defensive driving strategies to their fullest and retaining the speed to get away.

But as the hailstorm of bullets blew into the Blazer from all four sides, he decided he just might want to rethink that position.

The assault continued.

Lyons pressed his face against the Blazer's floorboards as his hands tried impotently to draw a weapon in the tight confines. Fragments of glass rained over his back, razor-edged shards biting into his skin. Other ragged pieces pierced his clothing and peppered his hair. Each time he raised his chest high enough to move his hand toward the Gold Cup .45, another burst of gunfire drove him back to the floor.

He changed tactics, trying to get the Colt Python out of the belt holster. But the Able Team leader's hip was lodged firmly against the seat, wedging the big revolver under the thumb-snap retainer.

A quick mental image of goldfish in a bowl flashed through Lyons's mind. Then the bowl became a barrel, and he saw men standing to the sides, shooting the fish with automatic rifles.

As the barrage continued, the ex-cop finally got his left hand under his coat and jerked the .45 free. His thumb lowered the manual safety to fire before returning to position.

More bullets pounded the Blazer. Lyons heard several rounds ricochet off the engine block under the hood. What was left of the windshield finally collapsed, and a new thunderstorm of glass poured over his back. Then the metal blew from the insides of the doors, and as he hugged the floor beneath it all again, Carl Lyons wondered exactly what good he thought getting the .45 out of the holster was going to do him. He couldn't even rise high enough to see over the sides of the car, let alone pick up a target.

To do so, he'd have to choose one of the four directions from which the assault was coming. And just as soon as he did, he'd be cut to ribbons by the other three.

The relentless pounding continued, no breaks, no hesitations, no pauses to change magazines. That meant one hell of a lot of gunmen stood circling the Blazer.

It suddenly dawned on Lyons that the time had finally come. He was about to die.

The Able Team leader's first reaction was to laugh, but just as quickly the laughter faded. Die facedown in a car? A gun in his hand and unable to put it to use? His mind flashed back to the goldfish in the barrel. No, Carl Lyons didn't think this was quite the way he intended to die. Oh, he might check out in the next few seconds, all right. Shuffle the hell right off this mortal coil. But if he did, he would go down fighting. This goldfish intended to shoot back.

The big ex-cop knew all that had saved him so far was that the enemy didn't know his exact location in the Blazer. He'd lose that advantage as soon as he fired his first rounds. He no longer cared. They—whomever "they" were—would get him sooner or later, and the first man who stuck his head into sight was going to precede Carl Lyons into the afterlife.

Ignoring the onslaught now, Lyons rose high enough to roll to his side. He felt the heat as several rounds skimmed an inch over his chest and head. He moved over to his back, dropping as low in the Blazer as possible as the attack went on.

He rested the Gold Cup across his chest as he waited. Finally short periods of silence began working their way through the automatic fire. The assault was almost over. He knew what would happen next. There would be a brief moment during which the gunmen would look at one another, wondering who would walk forward to check their handiwork.

Lyons didn't know who would draw the short straw.

Just that he'd kill whoever did.

Finally the gunfire stopped completely. Cautious footsteps padded across concrete toward the Blazer.

The Able Team leader felt a smile break on his face. Carl "Ironman" Lyons was prepared to face the Grim Reaper.

"The joke's on you, you hooded bastard," Lyons said out loud. "I've cheated your ass for years."

He flipped the safety off the Gold Cup.

A head appeared in the window, and his finger moved back on the trigger.

Stony Man Farm

AKIRA TOKAIDO GLANCED UP the ramp and saw Kurtzman busy at his console, then pulled the headphones over his ears and adjusted the volume on his CD player. As he turned back to his own computer screen, heavy metal blasted into his brain.

The yellow screen in front of his face flashed orange, then black as the new computer program digested the information he was feeding it.

Poisoning, Tokaido had just typed in. Potassium.

The young Japanese-American cracked his knuckles as a list of known deaths resulting from an intentional overdose of potassium began appearing down the screen. He hit the Home key twice, moving the cursor automatically to the end of the list. "Shit."

There were 2492 cases on the list. And that was only from the Interpol files.

The light on Tokaido's intercom button began to flash. Jerking the headphones off, the young man traded them for the receiver. "Yes, boss?" he said, turning to look up the ramp again.

"What's wrong?" Kurtzman asked.

"And what makes you believe there is something wrong?" Tokaido grinned. He knew Kurtzman had to have looked down and seen his reaction to the long list.

Kurtzman waited without answering.

"There are too many potassium poisonings on the list to be of any value to us," Tokaido finally said. "Before I could check on them all, the Huntsman will have died of old age."

"Then start with the ones during the past year," Kurtzman said. "If you don't find anything, move back another year. Then skip by twos."

Tokaido said his thanks and programmed the computer to give him a list of all the potassium poisonings during the past year. Moments later a shorter list appeared. This one contained only a few hundred cases, and Tokaido took a deep breath.

It would be a long and tedious process, like trying to fill the ocean with an eye dropper. The young computer whiz bent to the task.

Monaco

THE EXECUTIONER WAS a man of action, not idleness. He was a soldier, not a detective. But a certain amount of investigation sometimes became imperative in his war.

Before an enemy could be destroyed, he had to be identified.

Bolan took a seat at the end of the long conference table. He opened the first of a stack of manila file folders, then glanced up as his eye caught a figure entering the room.

A young woman in her mid-twenties stopped just inside the door. "Mr. Belasko," she said, "I am Sergeant Collette Delisle, from the intelligence division. The prefect has assigned me to act as your aide."

The Executioner nodded. "Grab a chair and a folder," he said.

Delisle slid into the seat next to him and took the top folder off the stack. "What are we looking for?" she asked.

"Coincidences. We've found a bunch so far, and I've got a feeling there are more. Look for patterns. Anything out of the ordinary that might have been missed five years ago." He paused, glancing over to the young sergeant. "Did you work the casino attack?"

The woman's face reddened slightly. "I have been with the force only three years," she admitted. "But we studied this case closely in the academy, and I have pursued it since being assigned to intelligence."

The question Bolan had wanted answered just had been. How old was Collette Delisle? She looked too young to be a sergeant. Of course the Executioner had seen far stranger things than young sergeants over the years, but considering her looks, there were two possibilities.

She was a whiz kid who'd been promoted fast because she deserved it, or her shapely legs and lovely features had caught the eye of Prefect LaSalle.

The Executioner shuffled through the bulky file, finding that it consisted primarily of interview report forms. The Monaco police had questioned hundreds of tourists after the terrorist attack, and each session had been documented in detail by the investigator.

Bolan started reading the interviews, looking for similarities in what the tourists had said. The reports were in French, which slowed him somewhat. He shook his head briefly in disbelief at the bureaucratic waste of words that slowed him even more.

Closing the file, the Executioner shoved it to his side and reached for the next folder on the stack. The interviews were long and monotonous, and the best bet was to leave them for last. Something might turn up in the other files.

As he opened the new file, Bolan glanced to his side. Collette Delisle sat studying a set of photographs from the file she had chosen. Her eyebrows had lowered in concentration.

Bolan's new folder contained a chronological series of investigative field reports that began with the account of the officers in the second squad car to arrive at the scene. The first paragraph told of the first officers to respond.

They had been promptly shot to death by the terrorists.

The warrior read through other reports, getting different facts, different viewpoints of the same situation. Several reports estimated the number of terrorists inside the building at twenty-five, but made no mention of where that number had come from. The Executioner also learned the details of the negotiations that had taken place before the authorities had given in to the terrorists' demands.

When he got to the report of the chief negotiator, Bolan frowned. The terrorists hadn't demanded the usual jet and buses to transport them to the airport. They had already arranged for their own departure— a Boeing 727 waiting at the airport. It had landed under other pretenses, and authorities hadn't connected it to the casino until the two buses—also ready and waiting—had been allowed through the police barricades to pick up the men inside the casino.

The buses had backed up to a rear fire exit of the building, loaded their passengers through back doors under the cover of darkness, then sped to the waiting 727.

Three minutes after the plane was in the air, the casino had exploded in flames. The remains of the hostages—all had been killed prior to the terrorists' departure—had been found in the ashes.

Bolan sat back and closed the file.

Delisle looked up. "Something?" she asked.

"Maybe. Anyone ever get an accurate account of the number of men involved in this strike?"

The sergeant shook her head, her long auburn hair whisking around her face. She moved it back with both hands, then said, "No. They were very careful that police did not see them board the bus, or transfer from the plane."

"So there's no way of knowing how many terrorists entered the casino and how many came out. Where did the investigators who wrote these reports come up with the twenty-five figure?"

"It was a number given by their spokesman during negotiations."

"Then it means nothing." Bolan glanced down at the file again. "And the buses. It says here that each one carried seats for over forty passengers. If they only had twenty-five men, didn't anybody wonder why the terrorists had brought two?"

Delisle nodded. "It was at first thought that they had more men than they had admitted."

"That doesn't make sense," Bolan said. "The number twenty-five came from their spokesman. If he was going to lie about their strength, he'd have told you he had more men than he actually had."

"Exactly," Delisle agreed. "It was finally decided during the follow-up investigation that the two buses were designed to split the terrorists up in case of an attack. You Americans have an expression I believe...." Her voice trailed off. She closed her eyes in thought, and Bolan watched her long fluttering eyelashes. When she looked up again, she smiled. "The eggs should not all be carried in the same basket?"

"Close enough."

"No, it is 'Don't put all of your eggs in one basket'. Yes, I distinctly remember Captain Greven telling me that when we spoke of this very thing. He said—"

"Wait a minute," Bolan said. "Greven told you this?"

The woman's lips pursed, and a quizzical look entered her sultry brown eyes. "Yes, did you know him? Captain Greven was a lieutenant of detectives five years ago. It was he who originally offered the theory that the men in the casino split into two buses in case of a counterattack. Why?"

Bolan didn't answer. Evidently the word that Greven had been dirty wasn't out among the troops yet. He saw no reason to get it started now. There might be other cops on the payroll of whoever was behind this, and the knowledge that Greven had been exposed would send them scurrying to cover themselves.

The Executioner grabbed another file from the stack and opened it.

When it became obvious Delisle would get no answer to her question, she did the same.

Bolan began poring over a stack of interrogations. They differed from the interview reports in tone. It quickly became obvious that the Monaco police had little to go on, and it had been a case of "round up the usual suspects" to cover the department politically.

The Executioner was halfway through the questioning of a recently released Italian burglar, wondering what possible connection the police could have thought he had to the casino incident, when he heard a muffled shriek.

Delisle looked up, her brown eyes flashing with excitement.

"What have you got?" Bolan asked.

She scooted her chair closer to his, turning the file toward him and spreading three more interview forms across the table. "I do not see how this could have been missed until now."

The warrior waited.

"This man," the sergeant said, tapping a page with a long fingernail, "Robert Slagel, an American. He had drinks with one of the victims, Jesse Garcia of Barcelona Personal Protection Products, the night before the casino attack. Garcia told Slagel he had been accompanied by his supervisor, Herme Lopez. They had both won the trip to Monaco in a contest sponsored by their company."

Bolan nodded. Lyons had already discovered the free trip connection. "Go on."

The woman's long red-nailed finger moved to another report. "In this interview, the bartender of Chez Paris—that's a bar down the street from the casino—tells of serving an English woman named Claudia Nichols. She had come in during the afternoon of the attack. Chez Paris was quiet, and they spoke extensively." The beautiful young sergeant paused. "Nichols told him she worked for a London-based private security agency. She was accompanied by a man whose name the bartender didn't remember, but he remembered that the man was white-haired, short and obese. And that he was her supervisor at the firm.

"This one," she went on, tapping the third report. "Same story, basically. A witness met victim Kurt Ostfeld, a security officer in Munich, and his supervisor... a short fat man with gray white hair. Both of them had won their trips, as well." The full red lips curled into a smile of triumph. "Three victims accompanied by their supervisors? Three free company-sponsored trips? I do not think so."

Bolan stood, studying the young woman. She might still have been promoted because of her looks, but if she had been, the Monaco police had gotten a damn good brain in the bargain. "I don't think so, either," he said. "Wait here. I'll be back in a few minutes." Leaving the conference room, he hurried down the hall.

The "coincidences" were still mounting up. First, all of the victims had a past record of spotty police work or military service. Then it turned out that the trips to Monaco had been prizes won by the victims. At least three of the victims had been accompanied by their supervisors who had also won company holidays.

And at least two of those supervisors sounded like the same short, fat, white-haired man.

Bolan entered LaSalle's outer office, nodded at the secretary and hurried past to the inner door. He found the prefect on the telephone.

"I will call you back." LaSalle hung up and turned to Bolan.

"I need to make another call," the Executioner said.

LaSalle sighed. He walked to the door and stopped, his hand on the knob. "When you are finished, may I assume you will tell me what is going on?"

"You may assume." Bolan picked up the phone and dialed Stony Man Farm as LaSalle left the office.

A moment later, Barbara Price lifted the phone.

"I've got more for Aaron to feed his magic machine," the Executioner said, explaining about the buses, then telling Price what Delisle had found about the victims' free trips and the supervisors. "And I want to know who owns three companies. Barcelona Personal Protection Products, Nightingale Security in London, and Munich's Alarm Systems Limited. My guess is that they'll all filter back to some parent company." He paused, then said, "And let's find out who owns all of the companies who employed the victims."

"Anything else?" Price asked.

Bolan told her about the similar descriptions of the two supervisors. "That part *could* simply be a coincidence," he said.

"There's more than one short fat man with white hair running around these days," Price agreed. "But in light of the rest... I'll get Aaron on it right now. Want Jack to start your way?"

"Affirmative, Barb. I've got a feeling this white-haired man is a key to the whole operation. As soon as we've IDed him, I'm going to find out just exactly what he knows."

"Striker?" Price said.

"Yeah?"

"I don't have to tell you to be careful, do I?"

"No."

"This thing is about to break," Price said. "I can feel it.

"That's right. And I'm going to make sure all hell breaks loose with it." He hung up.

The warrior walked slower on his way back to the conference room. Now came the hard part—waiting for both the Stony Man ID on the man with the white hair, and for Grimaldi to arrive.

Delisle had closed the files and stacked them by the time he reentered the room. She sat facing the door, her legs crossed at the knee.

The Executioner's gaze fell involuntarily as the woman's shapely thighs moved.

The woman was staring at him, an impish grin on her face. "Are we finished?" She paused, then added, "The files, I mean." Her double meaning was obvious.

Bolan nodded.

Delisle smiled. "I would be happy to buy you a drink."

"Love to," he said. "But I'll have to take a rain check. I've got a plane on the way."

The policewoman's eyebrows rose slightly. "Perfect. The place I had in mind is only three blocks from the airport. We could wait there."

Bolan chuckled. "Okay."

Delisle rose from her chair, cast a sly look his way and took his arm.

"This is a quiet place, I hope," the Executioner said as they left the room and started toward the nearest exit. "I'm tired, and right now the last thing I need is loud music and shouting."

"It can be quiet, or it can be loud. I will leave those details to you."

"I'm not sure I understand," he said. "What's the name of this place?"

The beautiful young sergeant squeezed his arm. "It is called simply Collette's apartment."

Italy

"WHEN YOU WERE still with Mossad, Yakov," Ranon Goldberg said, "I used to wonder sometimes where your loyalties would lie if put to the test." He stared into the eyes of his former partner. "If Israel should go to war with France, which country would you support?" It had been a rhetorical question, and without waiting for an answer, he glanced around the interior of the plane, his gaze moving from McCarter to Manning, then Encizo to James. With a quick final glance at Jabbar, he turned back to Katz. "Now, I see I must throw America's hat into the riddle, as well."

Manning spoke up before Katz could answer. "America? I'm from Canada."

"And I'm Cuban," Encizo added.

McCarter reached up, tipping the brim of his boonie hat. "Don't forget Her Majesty, Queen Elizabeth," he said in his strong Cockney accent.

Goldberg waved a hand in front of his face, dismissing the comments. "Yes, perhaps," he said. "But the United States is behind this ... this *thing* of yours, whatever it is."

Katz grinned at his old friend. "What makes you say that?"

Goldberg turned toward the Phoenix Force leader, and Katz could see the nervous sweat on his cheeks and upper lip. "Because," he said, "to quote a Yank expression, the U.S. is the only nation with 'balls big enough' to think they could get away with a secret team like this." He paused, and for a moment the hum of the engines was all that could be heard in the rear of the Israeli cargo plane. "Exactly who *do* you work for now, Yakov?"

Calvin James, the only American citizen in the crew, finally spoke up. "We could tell you, Ranon," the black warrior said with a grin, "but then we'd have to kill you."

Goldberg just shook his head.

The wheels of the plane touched down, and Katz and the other men of Phoenix Force rose to their feet, lifting their gear bags. They had already changed from battle dress to civvies, and now McCarter finally remembered his floppy cap and transferred it from his head to the side pocket of a briefcase.

A few minutes later, they were seated in a light blue Ford van and driving through the crowded streets of Naples.

Katz had taken the passenger's seat. He turned now, facing the other men in the back of the van. "Tell us again what you told our friend," he ordered Jabbar.

Jabbar wiped his forehead with the back of his hand. "There is an arms hijacking set to go down somewhere in the Naples area," he said. "The U.S. is closing the NAVSTA naval station there. The Italian government has purchased the small arms from the base and they are to be transported to an Italian army unit near Benevento."

The van left the city and started along the coastal road that bordered the Tyrrhenian Sea. Katz watched the waves drift in, breaking softly against the shore. Far in the distance, he could see the island of Capri. Its beauty seemed to stand in defiance of the violence the Israeli knew would soon take place in the area.

"Jabbar did not know exactly where they plan to hit the convoy," Goldberg went on. "Somewhere along the road."

Katz glanced to the informant, who shrugged.

The volcanic peak of Vesuvius appeared, rising above the shore just south of the city. Katz pulled a map from the pocket of his jacket. "I doubt they will strike along the coast," he said. "The sea eliminates one direction of potential escape."

"Unless they've got a boat," Encizo said.

Former Navy SEAL Calvin James shook his head. "They'd never get away in time. The Italian army is running the convoy, and they'll be on guard. They could radio the Navy and have them intercept any vessel the terrorists used. No, they'll take the guns and run inland. Find someplace to hide until the heat's off."

Katz nodded in agreement. His eyes scanned the coastal road anyway, looking for areas of potential ambush. There was another possibility. Sometimes the enemy did what appeared to be foolish, relying on the hopes that it would be unexpected.

Goldberg turned the van onto an inland highway, and they started over the rolling hills that led to Benevento. Lifting what appeared to be a simple beverage holder between the front seats, Phoenix Force's

Mossad contact revealed a hidden console and radio. "I must report to our people in Naples," he said, lifting the microphone. "They are expecting me."

Katz settled back against the seat as they continued through the Italian countryside. He listened to Goldberg speaking in Hebrew, yet could make out only part of the transmission. Many things had changed since he had left the Mossad, and of course the radio codes would have been modified almost daily.

As they neared the village of Benevento, Goldberg's face suddenly went white. His voice rose an octave, and then he signed off and dropped the microphone back into the console.

"What is it?" Katz asked.

He took a moment to respond, and when he finally answered, it was in the tired voice of an old man. "It is over."

"What is over?"

"The hijacking. They got the arms shipment just outside NAVSTA's front gate."

Katz drew in a deep breath. His suspicion that the hijackers might do the unexpected had come too late. They had bucked the odds, and the unexpected had paid off.

"That's not all. There was a brief gun battle, and during it the terrorists stopped a vehicle trying to enter the base. They pulled a woman from the car and took her hostage to effect their escape." He paused, finally looking up. "It was the daughter of the American rear admiral."

Katz didn't speak.

"In any case, I am to report immediately to the Naples Mossad headquarters. My superiors did not say it, but I suspect they think I am somehow involved with these crazed screaming Hunters or whatever they call themselves."

Adrenaline suddenly shot through Katz's system as if he'd been shocked with a stun gun. He had told Goldberg nothing about the Huntsman, but "Hunters" sounded a lot like the word. "What did you say?" the Phoenix Force leader demanded.

Goldberg shrugged, pointing to the radio. "One of the terrorists was mortally wounded during the gunfight," he said. "He mumbled something about Hunters who could not be killed . . . or some such gibberish."

8

Omaha, Nebraska

"Listen, Ironman," Schwarz said as he looked into the bullet-ridden Blazer, "I know my jokes aren't always that funny, but is that any reason to shoot me?"

Lyons let up on the trigger of the .45, flipped the safety back up with his thumb and wriggled up off the floorboard. "The thought's crossed my mind before," he growled.

Schwarz opened the door, more glass and a strip of metal trim falling from the vehicle as he did. He reached in, grasped Lyons's forearm and pulled him to the parking lot.

Behind Schwarz, the big ex-cop saw Blancanales pull the rented Oldsmobile across the lot, wheeling past the bodies of several downed gunmen who'd been caught from behind by the other two Able Team warriors. More gunmen, maybe two dozen in all, lay scattered around the demolished Blazer.

"How'd you know where to find me?" Lyons asked.

Schwarz laughed. "We got down to the café early. The gunfire was a little hard to miss." He paused, frowning as he stared down the street. "Which also means the cops should be on their way by now."

As if to confirm his statement, a siren sounded in the distance.

Blancanales pulled to a halt near the rear of the Blazer and jumped out, opening the trunk.

Lyons glanced quickly up and down the Blazer. Bullet holes dotted the vehicle like the spots on a leopard. The windshields—both front and back—and all four windows had been blown out, and steam hissed from under the hood.

The Blazer had served them well, but it had found its final resting place.

The Able Team leader hurried to the rear of the vehicle, letting Gadgets swing the tire rack out before inserting the key and unlocking the tailgate. Forming an assembly line between the two vehicles, they transferred their weapons and other equipment to the Oldsmobile. Pol slid behind the wheel again, with Lyons taking the passenger's seat as Schwarz dived into the back.

A moment later they were on the street, passing the first of the curious rubbernecks who were just now sticking their noses out from cover to see the damage.

"Go get 'em, boys," Schwarz said as they passed the flashing lights and wailing siren of the first squad car a block later.

Lyons hadn't had time to notice that Gadgets had already installed the portable programmable radio under the dash. But now he looked down as traffic came over the airwaves. "Stony Man Base to Able One. Come in, One."

Lyons lifted the mike to his lips as another police car raced past them in the opposite lane. "One here. Go, Stony."

Barbara Price's voice came back. "Location, Ironman?"

"Still in Omaha."

"Good. Pull off the dental visits for a while. Striker just called in with new Intel." She ran down what Bolan had learned in Monaco, ending with the similar descriptions of the "supervisors" who had won company trips. "I need you to interview some of the victims' surviving family members," the Stony Man mission controller said. "See if you can learn anything about who the victim's supervisor was."

Lyons frowned. "Why not just go to the companies themselves, Barb? They should know. The supervisors might still be working there."

Static crossed the airwaves for a second, then Price said, "If we don't get anything from the families, we'll have to. But it's beginning to look like the companies themselves might be in on whatever's going on."

The Able Team leader thumbed the mike again and said, "Affirmative. Got a list with addresses?"

"Yes, and the first one's right there in Omaha. Norman Hlabka. You can drive to it." She read the name of Hlabka's widow and gave an address.

"We're on our way," Lyons said and cradled the mike.

"It's over by the river," he told Pol.

Behind him, Lyons heard Gadgets unzip a nylon case as Blancanales turned, heading up the ramp to a thoroughfare in the general direction of the Missouri River. A moment later, the Able Team leader turned to see that Gadgets had pulled out the lap-top computer and called up a city map of Omaha on the screen.

"It's the next exit, Pol," Schwarz said.

Blancanales guided the Olds down the ramp.

Lyons glanced around. They were in a light-industrial section of Omaha's Czech community. Pol drove on, following Schwarz's orders, turning into a middle-income residential area.

Five minutes later, Pol pulled up in front of a split-level house covered with gray aluminum siding. Lyons opened the door. "Wait here," he said, and got out.

The Able Team leader fished the Justice Department credentials out of his jacket as he crossed the neatly trimmed lawn and mounted the steps to the porch. He knocked lightly on the door, using a brass knocker that sent tiny musical chimes inside the house, along with the dull thuds.

A moment later, a curtain in the picture window beside the door moved slightly.

Lyons held his open credential case up to the glass. "Mrs. Hlabka?" he said. "I'm Special Agent Johnson. May I speak with you?"

Slowly the door opened to the end of a brass chain. In the shadows through the crack, Lyons saw the wrinkled face of an old woman.

"What do you want?" Imogene Hlabka asked.

"I need to ask you a few questions."

"About Norman?"

"Yes, ma'am."

The face in the crack disappeared briefly. Lyons heard the chain come off, then the door opened again, wider this time. He stepped over the threshold into the living room.

And into the private hell of a hard-core chronic alcoholic.

The blended stench of stale wine, cigarette smoke, sweat and general squalor assaulted the big ex-cop's olfactory senses. Around him, he saw stack upon stack of old magazines and newspapers, their pages curling and yellowed with age. Particles of month-old, perhaps year-old, food had been trampled underfoot into the threadbare carpet. Empty wine bottles lay scattered across the floor. Half-empty glasses, filled with deep scarlet liquid, covered the scarred wood coffee table. Cigarette butts, smoked to their soggy brown filters, floated at the top of the grimy receptacles.

Imogene Hlabka stepped back from the door clutching the lapels of her stained housecoat. Her sunken eyes struggled to look up into Lyons's, and in them the Able Team leader saw one of the most profound sadnesses he had ever seen. He could also see that his estimate of her age had been wrong. Probably no older than thirty-five, her skin had wrinkled like that of a woman in her sixties.

"What can I tell you that I haven't told other policemen a thousand times already?" she asked.

Lyons noticed the slight slur in her speech. Not much, just enough to let him know that she'd had a few, and that having a few was a twenty-four-hour-a-day pastime. He pocketed the Justice Department credentials. "Do you remember much about your husband's job?" he asked.

A snicker escaped the woman's dried lips, which brought on a hacking cough. She reached into the pocket of her housecoat for a package of cigarettes and stuck one into her mouth. "I do my best not to remember much of anything anymore."

Lyons waited until the cigarette was lighted, then said, "Please try, Mrs. Hlabka. We might be onto something new that might help us finally find the men responsible for your husband's death."

Imogene Hlabka blew smoke out her nose, then looked back up at Lyons. For a moment, her faded irises cleared, and she said, "Would you like to sit down?" She made her way to the couch, flopped down and lifted what looked to Lyons like a jelly jar filled with wine.

He moved closer, but remained standing. "Try to remember your husband's supervisor, Mrs. Hlabka. Did you know him?"

Another snort brought another coughing fit. "Oh, I knew him all right. Gilbert Penny, you mean?"

Lyons shrugged. "I don't know, ma'am."

"Well, it would have to be. He was the only supervisor Norman ever had at the security company."

"What do you remember about Gilbert Penny?"

Imogene Hlabka took another gulp of wine and set the jar back down on the table. "Him trying to stick his hand up my skirt every time there was a company Christmas party, for one thing," she said. She stopped for a moment, then a new, even deeper sadness entered her sunken eyes. "I wasn't always the wine-soaked old hag you see before you now, Mr...."

"Johnson," Lyons said. "How old of a man was Gilbert Penny?"

"Oh, late fifties. Early sixties. Old enough to know better."

"What did he look like?"

"Oh, he was..." Her voice trailed off, then she said, "Norman often took pictures at the parties. Would you like to see them?"

"Very much," Lyons said. He glanced around the room, then at his watch. Finding anything in this mess could take years.

He was surprised when Imogene Hlabka stood, walked directly to a cabinet against the wall and pulled out a bound photo album. She resumed her place on the couch. A smile touched her lips as she opened the album, patted the seat next to her and said, "Please."

Lyons sat next to her, ignoring the stench of cat urine that wafted from the frazzled upholstery.

Imogene turned several pages, then stopped. "Oh! There we are the time we went to Las Vegas!"

Lyons glanced down to the photo. A man he assumed to be Norman Hlabka, wearing white duck pants and a loose sport shirt, smiled into the camera. His arm was draped around a beautiful woman whose long blond hair had caught the breeze, a few strands wrapping around her face. Her eyes sparkled with excitement. The woman bore only a faint resemblance to Imogene Hlabka—as if she might have been the wrinkled woman's daughter.

"I told you I was beautiful," she said. For a moment, the same sparkle Lyons had seen in the picture entered her eyes.

"Mrs. Hlabka, I know this has been difficult—"

"I know, I know," the woman said, turning pages in the photo album again. "You want to see Norman's supervisor." She came to a section of photos that showed men in suits and women in gowns, then tapped one of the pictures with her finger. "There he is. See? Coming up behind me. Probably getting ready to grab my ass."

Lyons couldn't stop the laugh that escaped his throat. In spite of the wretchedness to which Imogene Hlabka had allowed herself to sink, the woman had a certain charm about her. He stared at the picture.

Imogene was right. At one time, before her husband's murder, she had been something.

The anger started in Lyons's lower abdomen and worked its way up to his chest. The terrorists who had murdered her husband had killed Imogene Hlabka, too. They'd shattered the lives of many others.

The Able Team leader continued to study the picture. Imogene Hlabka stood facing the camera. Behind her, he saw a dark-skinned man approaching from behind. And the man's eyes *were* on her posterior.

"That's him?" Lyons asked.

"Yes. Wait, maybe there's a better picture of him." She turned another page, then said, "Yes," and pointed to the lower right-hand corner of the album. "There."

The same man now stood leaning against the bar, a plastic champagne glass in one hand. This time, he was trying to catch a peek down the low-cut neckline of a short brunette who stood talking to him.

Lyons studied the second picture as he had the first, remembering the description the Monaco witness had given of Hlabka's supervisor. Short and fat, with thick white hair.

The man Lyons saw now was short, but he could have never been called fat. And the only hair on his head was the brown tufts that shot out from around his ears. The rest of his head was as smooth as a cue ball.

"Mrs. Hlabka, are you sure Norman never had any other supervisor? Maybe a man with thick white hair?"

"Norman had only been with the company four years when he was killed, Mr. Johnson. He worked under Gilbert the whole time."

Lyons felt his blood begin to race. "Mrs. Hlabka, did Norman happen to take any pictures of his trip to Monaco?"

"Why, yes. I made him promise to. The trip he won didn't include spouses, and at first he refused to go by himself. I made him go, but made him promise he'd bring back pictures." She paused, tears filling her eyes. "They sent the film back with his things. He didn't want to go, I made him. *He didn't want to go...."*

Lyons reached out and took her hand. "I know it's painful, Mrs. Hlabka. But I very much need to see those pictures."

She rose slowly, pulling a stained handkerchief from another pocket of her housecoat and dabbing her eyes as she returned to the cabinet. When she returned, she held another photo album. She handed it to Lyons, lifted her wineglass and drained what remained.

Lyons opened the album as Mrs. Hlabka walked uncertainly out of sight into another room. He began skimming down the pages, seeing an assortment of pictures that showed Norman Hlabka in Monaco. The anger he felt at the terrorists who had not only killed the men and women in the casino, but destroyed the lives of their loved ones as well, came back when he recognized the stains on the plastic covering the photos.

Tears. The tears of a widow.

He stopped at a shot of Norman Hlabka in the lobby of the casino. Standing next to him, looking the other way, was a short fat man with white hair as thick as a teenager's. Lyons got two immediate impressions. First, it appeared that the white-haired man had realized that his picture was about to be taken at the last second, and looked the other way to avoid it.

The second impression Lyons got was that he knew the man.

The Able Team leader glanced up as Imogene Hlabka returned to the room, her glass full of wine once more. He frowned at the white-haired man.

Part of the fat man's face was still visible. Who was he? Where did Lyons remember him from? Something in the ex-cop's brain told him the memory stemmed from an old case—maybe an old arrest. He held up the picture. "Do you recognize this man?" he asked.

Imogene stopped next to the couch, squinted at the photo, then shook her head. She sat back down.

Lyons glanced at Mrs. Hlabka as she set her wineglass—nearly empty again—on the coffee table. "Mrs.—"

"Imogene. Call me Imogene, pleasshh." The slur had gotten stronger.

"Imogene, could I take this picture with me?" he asked.

The woman's eyes were closed. "If it will help you find the men who killed my Norman," she said. "You can take the whole...houshhhhh." Imogene's head fell to her chest.

Lyons reached out, gently nudging her awake. Her eyes opened, but now all of the sparkle he had seen before had been chased away by the haunting memories. "Imogene," the Able Team leader said, "come with me. Let me take you someplace where you can get some help."

A thin smile covered the woman's face. "I don't want help."

"You're killing yourself," Lyons said.

The smile widened. "Yes, and soon I'll be with Norman." Her eyed closed again.

Lyons placed his hand gently on her forehead, opening the lids once more. "Imogene," he said bluntly, "would Norman have wanted you to drink yourself to death?"

The answer was a long time coming. But finally, Imogene Hlabka shook her head. "No."

The big ex-cop stood and helped her to her feet. He locked the front door behind them, then led the woman toward the Oldsmobile.

Nassau

"REVEILLE, SARGE," Jack Grimaldi said in a loud voice. "We're on our way down."

Bolan opened his eyes, hearing the roar of the plane engines drop to a hum as they descended over Nassau, Bahamas. He shifted in his seat, stretching his arms and legs.

The wheels touched down and Grimaldi taxied along the tarmac.

"By the way, Barb radioed again while you were asleep. Hal's got you cleared through customs."

Bolan nodded, glancing through the windshield to see a man walking toward the plane wearing the red slacks and white tunic of a Bahamas police officer. "You off again?"

Grimaldi shrugged. "Not unless they call me. You have your walkie-talkie?"

"Yeah." He opened the door and stepped down onto the tarmac.

The man in the tunic walked the Executioner quickly through customs, shook his hand, then hurried away. Ten minutes later, Bolan was leaving the airport in a rented Buick Skylark.

Refreshed from the sleep he'd caught during the flight, the warrior reviewed what Price's last radio transmission had told him.

Lyons had come up with a picture that appeared to be the white-haired man mentioned in the Monaco police reports. But he hadn't been anyone's supervisor as the reports had indicated. Faxed copies to Stony Man had resulted in a computer comparison with Kurtzman's magic machines, measuring jaw length and angle, shoulder slope and other physical elements.

The man in all three pictures was the same.

Bolan drove through the busy traffic of downtown Nassau, finally leaving the city's eastern border.

So the white-haired man had been matched again. But identifying him had remained, a process that would have proved lengthy even for Kurtzman's computers.

But Carl Lyons had beaten the computers this time. The big ex-cop had half recognized the man with the white hair, finally tying the vague memory back to an insurance scam he had worked over ten years ago as an L.A. detective. From there it had been a simple matter of Kurtzman tapping into LAPD files, then reading the names mentioned in the case over the phone to the Able Team leader.

The man was Charles Merwick Meritt. Meritt had turned out to be a highly successful international confidence man. There were no current warrants, but Interpol had him currently listed as living east of Nassau.

Following the directions Kurtzman had gleaned from the Interpol linkup, the Executioner turned toward the sea at the next crossroads. He bumped along a washboard gravel road for two miles before seeing the three-story house facing the beach and glistening blue water.

Bolan slowed, unzipped the overnight bag and pulled out the cellular phone. He activated the bat-

tery-powered scrambler, and a moment later he had
Price on the line. "Leo get through?" he asked.

Leo Turrin was Stony Man Farm's own answer to a
confidence man. Widely known in Mob circles as Leo
The Pussy, Turrin had promised to contact Meritt and
arrange an appointment for Bolan.

"He did," Price said. "Meritt knew who he was, all
right, and knew he'd better listen if he didn't want the
wrath of the Mafia to come down on him." She
paused. "Meritt's expecting a man fitting your description named Vince Styles. You're supposed to have
a joint venture between Leo and Meritt in mind that'll
be one hell of a score for both."

"Oh, I do, Barb," the Executioner said. "I do. It
just won't be a fifty-fifty partnership." He dropped
the phone back in his bag and turned off the gravel
onto a drive that led to a stone wall.

An iron gate stood across the drive, a small guard
shack next to it. Bolan stopped next to the shack as a
man carrying a clipboard stepped down from the tiny
building. He wore dark green slacks and a baggy fisherman's shirt, but Bolan saw the bulge behind his right
hip.

"Mr. Styles to see Mr. Meritt," the warrior said as
the man walked forward.

"Ah, yes." The guard looked down at his board.

The gate opened and Bolan drove through.

Charles Merwick Meritt's three-story white brick
home looked out of place as a beach house, and Bolan knew instinctively that the international con man

had wanted it that way. Beneath the carefully manufactured "front" of most of the world's most successful swindlers lay an ego in perpetual battle for the recognition a double life denied. That drive to be noticed came out in peculiar ways, and it appeared that Meritt's had expressed itself in the tall white columns, provincial shutters and doors, antebellum gazebos and the other outbuildings that scattered the grounds.

The Executioner pulled into a circular drive, stopping in front of the main door. He was met by a man who might have been the gate guard's twin brother. The similarities included the gun bulge under the fisherman's shirt.

"I park your car, mon."

Bolan shook his head. "I won't be that long."

"But Mr. Meritt, he say—"

A glance from the Executioner stopped the man in midsentence.

The warrior walked briskly up the steps, then knocked on the door. It was answered by another servant. "Mr. Meritt, he wait in the library."

Bolan noticed a slight tremble in his voice. The man was nervous. Had Merrit told him that Vince Styles represented the Mafia, or was there another reason for the fluttering speech?

His defense system on sudden alert, Bolan followed the man from the anteroom down a long hall, passing several closed doors.

The Executioner glanced over his shoulder. He could see no one in the hall, but he could sense a presence.

Bolan's hand fell to his belt buckle, the thumb hooking nonchalantly inside his waistband, his fingers now in position to draw either the Beretta or the Desert Eagle.

The man ahead of him stopped at another closed door at the end of the hall. The Executioner noticed his hand trembling as he reached for the doorknob. An ambush was imminent.

The warrior flung back the tail of his sport coat as the guide twisted the doorknob, then dived for the floor. Drawing the Desert Eagle with his right hand, Bolan dropped to one knee. His left hand curled up under his armpit, wrenching the Beretta from shoulder leather, his thumb inside the trigger guard.

The door in front of Bolan swung open to reveal two men aiming Heckler & Koch MP-5s down the hall. Dual bursts of gunfire sailed over the Executioner's head—chest-level had he still been standing.

A door opened behind him.

The Executioner fired twice, the big .44 Magnum pistol ripping passages through the chest cavities of the gunners in the doorway. At the same time, the index finger of his left hand dropped the Beretta's selector to 3-round burst. Raising the weapon over his shoulder, he drilled a blind trio of sound-suppressed 9 mm slugs down the hall to his rear. Three soft coughs reverberated against his ear.

The two men in front of him went down like timber to a chain saw. The Executioner twisted, throwing himself into a sitting position against the wall opposite the cringing doorman. Focusing straight ahead, he used his peripheral vision to watch both directions.

A man had fallen to his rear, at least one round of the blind burst finding its target. But as he watched, two more doors opened along the hall.

And out of the other corner of his eye, he saw a man wearing a blue T-shirt and jeans step over the bodies of the gunmen with the MP-5s. The man raised a large nickel-plated revolver.

The Executioner raised both weapons, the Desert Eagle aimed toward the front of the house, the Beretta through the door to the library, and pulled both triggers simultaneously.

The first .44 Magnum hollowpoint round found the throat of a gunner wielding a sawed-off Ithaca pump gun and took him out of play.

Another 3-round burst from the Beretta stitched a line up the blue T-shirt, from navel to sternum. The shiny S&W Model 29 fell to the carpet.

Bolan's second Magnum slug sailed over the descending body and drilled through the lower abdomen of a man gripping a stainless steel Ruger Mini-14. The man's mouth opened wide in a silent "Oh" of surprise before he crumpled to the floor in a limp heap.

The gunfire ended as abruptly as it had begun. As the explosive echoes off the narrow walls died down,

Bolan heard the whimpering of the doorman, hug-ging the wall across from him. The Executioner leaped to his feet. Shoving the barrel of the Desert Eagle against the back of the man's head, he patted him down for weapons but came up with nothing.

The warrior reholstered the Beretta. Why had he been attacked? Turrin had told Meritt that Vince Styles was a mafioso with a score for him. Surely the con man wouldn't take it upon himself to go gun-on-gun against the Mob.

No way. The answer had to be that Charles Mer-wick Meritt had been tipped off that the man calling himself Vince Styles would be an impostor.

Bolan grasped the doorman's shoulder, spun him and jammed the Desert Eagle against his jaw. "Be-fore we were so rudely interrupted," the Executioner said, "I believe you were taking me to see Mr. Mer-itt."

The man's jaw fell slack.

The warrior spun the man again, shoving him over the bodies in the doorway to the library. The man tripped, sprawling over the pile. When he'd struggled to his feet, he looked down at his hands, found them covered with blood and started to scream.

The Executioner stepped over the bodies and back-handed the man with the barrel of the Desert Eagle. The doorman's eyes closed as he slumped back to the carpet, unconscious.

Charles Meritt's library looked more like a public rather than a private collection of literature. Steel bookshelves lined the walls, as well as running through the center of the room to form a network of aisles. Here and there, couches, chairs and reading tables had been worked into the design.

Bolan turned to his left. A short fat man with thick, carefully blow-dried hair sat frozen in a leather chair next to one of the shelves. A leather-bound book lay open in his lap.

The warrior walked slowly to the man, stopping a foot in front of the chair. "You knew I wasn't Mob, didn't you?"

A tense smile played at Meritt's lips. He didn't answer.

Bolan brought around the barrel of the Desert Eagle, touching it between the man's eyes.

"Please...." he pleaded.

Bolan raised the gun again. "I asked a question. I expect an answer."

The Executioner dropped the magazine from the Desert Eagle and replaced it with a fresh load from his belt.

"Yes!"

"Who tipped you off?"

Meritt started to speak when Bolan saw his eyes suddenly flicker toward the doorway. Whirling, he saw that the doorman had regained consciousness, found one of the fallen subguns and turned it toward the Executioner.

Bolan and the doorman fired simultaneously.

A 3-round burst sailed to the Executioner's side as Bolan's double tap of hollowpoints caught the man in the chest and throat, driving him to his back. The warrior paused momentarily, making sure the man was dead. "I asked who tipped you—" he said as he swung the .44 back toward Meritt.

The Executioner stopped in midsentence. There was no need to waste his words.

Charles Merwick Meritt sat wide-eyed in death, three 9 mm holes pumping blood from his chest.

9

Italy

Calvin James leaned across the seat of the van and slapped Jabbar hard across the face with his left hand. His right drew the Spyderco Civilian knife from his belt, and the blade snapped open with a hard metallic thud. As he leaned across the seat, he felt the bandage around his ribs pull tighter.

James ignored it. The bullet that had skinned across his belly had done no serious damage. It would pain him for a few days, but it was no big deal.

The Phoenix Force warrior pressed the blade into Jabbar's throat, hooking the curved point just under the Adam's apple.

Goldberg pulled the van to the side of the road and turned to the rear. He started to speak, but Katz reached out, grasping his arm.

Katz shook his head. "Wait."

James's dark eyes drilled holes through Jabbar's. "You knew about this, didn't you," he growled in a low menacing voice. "You knew they'd be hitting the arms shipment outside the gate."

Jabbar started to shake his head, then stopped abruptly as the knife bit into his throat.

"I suggest you reply verbally. If you shake your head or nod, you'll be cutting your own throat."

Jabbar's eyes opened so wide James could see white all the way around the dark brown irises. "I knew...a little more than I told you."

James felt the anger rise in his throat. Before, threatening the Arab terrorist with the knife had been an act to convince him to talk. But now, someone had been kidnapped. Jabbar could have prevented that by coming clean to the Mossad or Phoenix Force.

"What will they do with her?" the Phoenix Force commando asked.

Jabbar's breaths came in short, jerky spasms. "If they know who she is, they will hold her and demand ransom."

"And if they don't?"

"They will kill her when she is no longer of any use."

James turned to the front seat.

Katz opened the console, retrieved the mike and handed it to Goldberg. "Call your people," he said. "The girl's identity must be made public immediately."

The Mossad agent nodded and took the mike.

As he spoke over the radio, James turned back to Jabbar. "Where will they take her?" he demanded.

"I do not know."

"Where will they take her!" James repeated.

"Please, I am not certain," Jabbar said in a weak, timid voice. His wide eyes tried to look down at the blade against the soft flesh of his throat. "But there is another safehouse in Rome. Perhaps there."

Goldberg finished with the radio transmission and dropped the mike back into the console. "I explained. They will see that it is done."

"Good," Katz said. "Let's hope it buys her enough time for us to get to Rome."

The Mossad operative nodded, threw the van into Drive and cut a sharp U-turn across the road. He floored the accelerator, and they started back toward the intersection where they'd turned earlier.

James leaned back, taking the knife away from Jabbar's throat. The terrorist's hand rose to his neck. He checked it for blood, then looked back across the van.

Katz turned in his seat. "You are not finished talking. Tell us everything you know about the safehouse." He paused. "If I even suspect you are lying, or holding anything back this time, I will turn you back over to my friend here. He had a year of medical school, and I am sure he would like to brush up on his surgery techniques."

Jabbar's eyes flashed back to James, who still held the open knife. James returned the stare, and Jabbar's gaze fell to his lap. "It is in a hidden room within a mosque. All who enter must do so through the mosque itself."

Katz rarely cursed, but he did so now. "Bullshit. How are they going to get the hostage in without drawing attention?"

"I have heard of a secret entrance, it is true," Jabbar said quickly. "But only those higher than myself are aware of its location. I swear by God this is true."

"That makes me feel *so* much better," Katz said.

The sun was setting by the time the southeast edge of Rome appeared in the distance. Goldberg slowed as traffic grew thicker. Then, following Jabbar's directions, he guided the van into the ancient city, passing first the Colosseum, then the Roman Forum before turning onto Via del Corso and fighting through the traffic near the Trevi Fountain. They cut down a side street for several blocks to the Spanish Steps, turned onto Via del Pinciana and found the mosque a block later, across from Rome's Zoological Gardens.

As Goldberg drove past, James pressed his face against the glass of the rear window, squinting through the dusk at the line of robed men waiting to enter the mosque. At the top of the steps that led to the front door, he saw several bearded men in turbans: mujahedeen, Muslim religious warriors. He could see no visible weapons, but James knew the baggy robes and muslin vests might hide everything from krises to Kalashnikovs.

The mujahedeen were herding the worshipers through a short archway.

James leaned across the van again, grasping Jabbar by the collar. "They're using a metal detector. Why didn't you say so?"

"I did not know!"

Goldberg's voice drifted from the front of the van. "There have been recent counterattacks upon Muslims by a Christian group here in Rome," he said. "One mosque was dynamited. Another machinegunned. The metal detector is no doubt a recent development."

"For whatever reason," Katz said, "it presents problems." The Israeli cleared his throat and reached into his pocket for a cigarette. "All of us gaining entrance without drawing attention was going to be hard enough the way it was. Now..." His voice drifted off as he lighted the cigarette.

Goldberg continued past the mosque, driving the length of the Zoological Gardens before leaving the street for a parking lot, where he turned around. "The situation is much like the one you told me about in Nazareth, Yakov," he said. "We will be lucky to get *one* man in to locate the hidden room. And he will have to be unarmed."

"Not necessarily," Calvin James said. He pulled a nylon gear bag from under the seat and set it in his lap. "I missed out on all the fun at the Evaluation Center." He unzipped the bag and began to rummage through the contents. "Now its my turn." Locating the small leather packet he sought at the bottom of the bag, James pulled it out. "Say hello to Mr. Karim

Abdul Fallah, formerly known as Kitwana." He opened the packet and looked inside. When he spoke again, his accent had changed to that of southern Africa. "A citizen of Botswana, I'm finally making my pilgrimage to Mecca."

Katz grinned at him. "So why are you here in Rome, Kitwana?" the Phoenix Force leader asked.

James met his eyes. "I just stopped off to pray at the mosque up the street."

Omaha, Nebraska

THE DENTAL ARTS BUILDING sat on the corner of Wilkens and Featherstone, six blocks from the city's South Side Mall. Seated in the Oldsmobile's passenger's seat, in the parking lot of the supermarket across the street, Carl Lyons watched the Omaha PD car drive by.

"He's got a small patrol area," Blancanales said from behind the wheel. "That's three times in the past hour and a half."

Lyons nodded. "And forty to forty-five minutes in between. Almost clockwork." He blew air between his clenched teeth as the black-and-white disappeared around a corner a block away. "Damn bad police work, running a predictable patrol like that." He paused. "But damn lucky for us." He turned halfway in his seat in time to see Gadgets Schwarz nod his agreement.

"The alarm system must be around back," Schwarz said. He lowered the binoculars. "There's a lead wire running through the door. I suspect it covers the windows, too. But the main unit has to be in the alley, 'cause I don't see it."

Lyons nodded. "That's better anyway," he said. "More cover." He closed his eyes and rubbed the lids. The lack of sleep was beginning to catch up with him.

"Let's give it another five minutes," the Able Team leader said. "It'll have gotten darker by then. Then we'll go. Gadgets, you come with me and take care of the alarm. Pol, I want you standing by behind the wheel just in case our exit has to be fast."

The other two members of Able Team nodded.

Lyons closed his eyes again, reviewing the events of the day and the previous night. Imogene Hlabka had been checked into a local hospital and registered for an alcohol-abuse program. She'd be in "detox" first, and Lyons knew she was in for a rough few days. She'd already entered withdrawal before Lyons left, but had managed to make her mind work long enough to give him the rest of the information he needed.

Before getting onto the dental-insurance program provided with his security job, Norman Hlabka's dentist had been a Dr. Edward Mayfield. Mayfield owned the dental-arts building, where he and seven other dentists practiced their trade. Lyons, still posing as Agent Johnson, had visited Mayfield that afternoon.

Yes, Norman Hlabka had been his patient for several years. And yes, Dr. Mayfield still had a set of Hlabka's dental records.

No, he wouldn't turn them over to Agent Johnson. That would take a court order, since Mayfield feared legal reprisal if he gave out personal patient information. And no, neither the Justice Department credentials nor the fact that the patient had been dead for five years meant jack shit to Dr. Mayfield.

The big ex-cop had gritted his teeth, fighting the urge to drive his fist through Mayfield's pompously grinning face. Instead, he had thanked the doctor for his time, promised to return with the required court order and left.

Well, Lyons had returned, and he'd brought his court order. He glanced down at his feet.

Of course, most people would call the court order he'd brought a boot.

He pulled the radio headset out of his jacket and slipped it over his ears. Flipping the switch on the main unit hidden on his belt, he tapped the mouthpiece in front of his face and heard the scratch come over the programmable unit plugged into the cigarette lighter. "Let's go, Gadgets," he said, glancing down at his watch. "We'll play it safe—give ourselves no more than thirty minutes inside. That should be more than enough time to find Hlabka's file."

Gadgets nodded. The two men exited the vehicle.

Lyons led the way across the street to the rear of the building. He made his way through the shadows along the alley, maneuvering around trash cans and air-conditioning condensers to the rear exit.

Turning, he stood watch as Schwarz pulled a set of wire cutters from inside his jacket and snipped the proper alarm wires. As soon as Gadgets had turned back to Lyons and nodded, the Able Team leader raised his black leather "court order" and kicked the door.

Following Schwarz through the opening, Lyons found himself in a small hallway. At the far end, he could see the glass of the front windows, and the Oldsmobile parked across the street. Closing the door behind him, the big ex-cop found that the clasp still caught. He whispered into the mouthpiece. "Can you copy, Pol?"

"Loud and clear."

"Roger. Keep us informed on the situation outside." Taking the lead, Lyons hurried down the hall, turning into the large office with the filing cabinets he'd spotted on his earlier visit.

Dim light from both the moon and streetlights flowed through the windows along the top of the wall, half illuminating the office. The Stony Man warriors pulled miniflashlights from their pockets for additional lighting.

"Take the right," Lyons whispered. Schwarz nodded and moved away.

The big ex-cop turned to the first large cabinet on his left, shining the flashlight onto the name tags on the drawers. "Damn."

Blancanales heard it over the airwaves. "What's wrong?" he asked.

"Nothing, Pol. Just that the records are filed by patient number rather than alphabetized. It means it's going to take a hell of a lot longer."

"No, it isn't," Schwarz whispered. Lyons heard him both over the radio and from the other side of the room. "Come here, Ironman."

Lyons turned and hurried around a desk in the middle of the room. He saw Gadgets standing before an open drawer in a file cabinet, shone his light down on the tag and saw Past Accounts.

Schwarz dug though the drawer with both hands, holding his flashlight in his teeth. "Bingo," he said, pulling out a thick file. "Norman Kelso Hlabka." He flipped through the contents, and Lyons saw a series of X-ray reports and other papers.

"Pol, we're coming out," Lyons said into the throat mike.

The Able Team leader twisted off the flashlight and returned it to his pocket. He was getting the eerie feeling he often got when things went too well, too smoothly. He glanced at his watch. They had been inside the building less than five minutes. It seemed too good to be true.

And it was.

The room was suddenly illuminated with overhead light, and both Lyons and Schwarz spun to see an old man wearing a security guard uniform standing in the doorway to the hall. The man looked to be seventy years old. His uniform hung loosely from his shoulders, his eyes were as red as blood, and a distinct odor of alcohol emanated from him across the room.

The four-inch Taurus .38 Special in his hand wavered nervously as he tried to train it on both men at the same time.

Lyons froze in his tracks. There had been no indication that the building employed a night watchman. The man had to have come in before they had set up their surveillance. He hadn't passed in front of any of the open windows since they'd arrived, or turned any lights on that hadn't been on all along.

But the answer wasn't that difficult to come by, considering the man's drunken state. The man probably had a little hole-in-the-wall someplace in the building where he set up bar each night then drank until he passed out.

"Keep your hands up," the old man slurred.

Out of the corner of his eye, Lyons saw Schwarz grin. "You didn't tell us to put them up, yet," Gadgets said. "How can we keep them up?"

"Put 'em up," the old man said. "Then keep 'em up." He swayed slightly.

Lyons glanced at Schwarz. Gadgets shrugged, then both men raised their hands into the air.

The old man frowned slightly, as if trying to decide what to do next. A moment went by. Then two.

Lyons hesitated. The situation was far more dangerous than it looked. The old man was drunk and scared, and he might pull the trigger accidentally at any time. They had to get him disarmed and out of the way as soon as possible, and they had to do it without hurting him.

When the old man failed to speak, Lyons finally did. "Now you should tell us to turn around," he said softly. "To keep our hands up, and don't try anything funny."

The security man nodded. "Turn around. Keep 'em up. Nothing funny, or I'll plug you."

As they turned, Lyons and Schwarz faced each other momentarily. A look of disbelief covered Gadgets's face. Silently he mouthed, "Plug you?"

"What now?" the old man said as soon as they'd turned.

"Better make sure we don't have any weapons," Schwarz replied.

"Yeah." Another long pause followed, then the old man's voice grew impatient. "Well? Do you?"

To his side, Lyons saw Schwarz's chest begin to jerk as the electronics man struggled to keep his laughter inside. "No, we don't have any weapons," Gadgets said. "But we might be lying, so come frisk us."

"Oh, yeah."

Lyons heard the old man's feet shuffle up behind him. Then, in his ear, he heard Blancanales. "Ironman, what's wrong?"

Lyons didn't answer. A moment later, he felt the barrel of the .38 press into his spine. He waited until the old man's hand began feeling around his belt, then turned and swept the revolver out of the drunken man's hand.

The old drunk took a step back, his eyes struggling to focus on the man who had just disarmed him. Before that could happen, Schwarz had moved in and jerked the handcuffs from the man's belt. Gadgets guided him gently down into a chair and cuffed his hands through the rungs behind his back.

"Hey, wait a minute...."

Lyons reached up, jerking the clip-on tie from around the man's throat. A moment later, the security guard had been gagged.

"Ironman," Blancanales said. "I've got a squad car creeping down the street out here. Where the hell are you?"

Lyons cursed under his breath. The old man had to have had a moment of lucidity and called the cops before confronting them.

"We're still inside," Lyons replied. "What's the car doing now?"

"Pulling up at the office building next door. There are two of them. They're getting out and starting your way."

Lyons swore again. The cops wouldn't be drunk, old or stupid. There was only one chance.

"Pol, watch them through the binoculars," Lyons said. "How are they acting?"

After a moment, Blancanales said, "About half-serious about the whole deal."

Lyons let out a breath of relief. That meant the local cops probably answered routine scare calls from the old security guard. That gave Able Team an edge. Not much of an edge, but the only one they were likely to get.

"They're splitting up," Blancanales whispered. "One's going to the back."

"Any sign of backup?"

Another pause. Then, "Not so far."

"Okay, Pol," Lyons said. "Here's what I want you to do." He went on to explain the impromptu plan he had just devised. "And make sure you lay enough rubber to get their attention."

"The plan's got holes, Ironman."

"You got a better idea, I'm all ears," Lyons came back.

"No."

The Able Team leader glanced at Schwarz. Leaving the drunken security guard to struggle halfheartedly against his restraints, they moved back down the hall to the alley door. A moment later, they heard the screech of tires in front of the dental clinic.

Through the back door, someone said, "Shit!" Then footsteps ran away across the pavement.

Lyons grasped the doorknob and waited.

"I'm turning into the alley right now," Pol's voice said in Lyons's ears.

"Where are they?"

"On the side of the building, both of them now, running toward me," Blancanales said. "They'll never get back to their vehicle in time."

"It's not pursuit I'm worried about, Pol," Lyons said. "It's bullets."

"Then be ready, Ironman. It's going to be close."

Lyons waited another second, then threw open the door. As he did, he heard the tires squeal again as Pol braked the car to a halt.

The big ex-cop sprinted out into the alley as Pol reached over the seat, opening the back door of the Oldsmobile.

From halfway down the alley, the Able Team leader heard the word, "Stop!" Diving into the back seat, he pulled his legs up under him, and a split second later felt Schwarz dive on top of him.

"We've got to stop meeting like this," Schwarz said as the Oldsmobile took off again down the alley. "People will talk."

Nassau

THE EXECUTIONER STARED at Charles Meritt in disgust. The doorman's bullets had missed him, but had found their mark in the little fat man. Now, the chance of learning the link the international con man had played in the Huntsman situation was gone forever. At least from Meritt's lips.

The warrior holstered the Desert Eagle. Where did he go from here? Until Stony Man came up with another lead, he seemed to have met a dead end.

Running footsteps suddenly sounded behind him. The Executioner whirled toward the door.

As his hand returned to the Desert Eagle, a tall, burly man with a handlebar mustache sprinted through the door, gripping a Glock 21 in his right hand.

The first shot from the Glock exploded as Bolan drew the Desert Eagle.

The .45 round caught the shoulder pad in his jacket, ripping the material away from his arm and sending a snowstorm of white lining floating over the Executioner's head. Bolan saw the gunner's hand ride the recoil, then start to bring the weapon back down.

The warrior threw himself backward over Meritt's corpse, the back of his calves striking the dead man and sending both body and chair tumbling to the floor. The second shot from the Glock thudded into Meritt as Bolan rolled to his side, diving behind a bookshelf.

Two more rounds struck the front of the shelves, sending books flying out the other side. Bolan rolled again, rising to a squatting position and moving farther into the labyrinth of bookshelves. Steel twanged as another .45 hit the metal beneath a row of volumes.

Bolan ducked around a corner, moving deeper into the room. The man with the Glock had been familiar—not his looks, but something about his manner-isms.

As yet another .45 exploded from the center of the room, Bolan realized the gunner had the same dead-eye look in his eyes as the other incarnations of the Huntsman.

A volley of semiauto gunfire peppered the book-shelves, the Huntsman firing blindly, "spraying and praying," hoping a wild round would find its way through the maze of bookshelves to its mark. Bolan counted the shots, adding to those already fired. With one in the chamber and a full magazine, the Glock 21 carried fourteen rounds. So far, eight had been ex-pended.

The Executioner moved slowly, cautiously, as he tried to pick up the direction from which the shots came. He moved faster each time he saw the flash of a green shirt round the corner of one of the aisles, staying a split second ahead of the bullets. He contin-ued to count the shots fired, hoping against hope that he might have the Huntsman in position to attack when the weapon finally ran dry.

Finally only one .45 remained in the Huntsman's weapon.

Bolan didn't kid himself. He knew there was a bet-ter than even chance that he would be the one to die in this deadly game of cat and mouse. But it was time to capture a Huntsman alive.

The Executioner moved forward, then stopped as he heard a soft snap, then a whooosh. He knew what it meant.

The Huntsman had reloaded. He was back to fourteen .45s.

Bolan had been lucky so far—lucky enough to avoid the thirteen rounds that had tried to kill him. But that luck wouldn't last forever. He had to move now.

Backing against a shelf away from the sounds, the warrior waited.

A moment later, he heard soft footsteps on the other side of the shelf he faced. He dropped silently to all fours, waiting, priming himself.

The footsteps drew parallel on the other side of the wall of books.

The Executioner drove forward like a defensive tackle coming off the line. His shoulder struck the bookshelf, and he felt the pain shoot down his arm as the hard steel dug against muscle and bone.

The heavy bookshelf teetered briefly, then toppled toward the Huntsman.

Bolan dived on top of it as .45-caliber explosions blasted past him, tossing books into the air at his sides. The Executioner knew he would have only seconds now before the Huntsman regained his bearings and shot him . . . or spouted his litany and stuck the gun in his own mouth.

The warrior heard a scream of anguished frustration as he flung books aside. "The Huntsman cannot die!" the man roared.

Bolan scooped more books aside, and the Huntsman's face suddenly appeared between two of the metal shelves. The thick square barrel of the Glock moved toward his open mouth.

The Executioner reached through the bookshelf, his right hand moving over that of the man on the floor. As the gun barrel passed the Huntsman's lips, he wedged the tip of his little finger into the narrow space between the Glock's trigger and the rear of the trigger guard.

The man squeezed the trigger and the warrior felt the sharp pinch on his fingernail. The Glock remained silent.

"The Huntsman cannot die," the man with the handlebar mustache mumbled around the barrel.

Bolan drove his left fist into the Huntsman's jaw.

"And this time," the Executioner promised, "he's not going to."

10

Rome, Italy

Calvin James had been a fighter from the time he was born. As a tough kid on Chicago's South Side, he had learned to fight with sticks, stones and fists. But his specialty had always been the edged weapon.

The tight bandage around his midsection seemed to cut him in two as James walked slowly down the street toward the mosque. He knew the secret to knife fighting was training. An accomplished blade man learned his skills, perfected them, then continued to practice. Otherwise, the razor-edged sharpness—both of knife and technique—dulled quickly.

James turned the corner, and the central dome and balconies atop the minarets of the mosque appeared. Ahead, he saw the line of men waiting to pass through the metal detector, and his right hand fell into the pocket of his robe. His fingers curled around one of the small wooden fléchettes.

When you reached Calvin James's level of knife-fighting expertise, competition became hard to come by. The other men at Stony Man Farm—particularly

Bolan and Blancanales—provided him with a damn good workout. But occasions when the schedules of Able Team, Phoenix Force and the Executioner coincided at the Farm were few and far between. And when they did, the three attack forces were usually too busy planning a mission to afford time for blade practice.

So, as part of his ongoing training, Calvin James had attended a recent knife-fighting seminar held in Hell's Canyon, Idaho. Called the Riddle of Steel, the seminar had attracted some of the world's top blade men and given James an opportunity to tune technique against opponents near his own caliber. But best of all, he had been introduced to a new weapon, one that now just might mean the difference between success and failure of the mission.

The Phoenix Force warrior pulled his hand from his pocket as he neared the steps. Using a metal detector didn't necessarily preclude a body search, and he wanted nothing to draw attention his way—particularly to his pockets.

Taking his place at the end of the line, James dropped his gaze and closed his eyes, affecting a prayerful demeanor. The other men did the same, shuffling forward each time the line moved.

Three minutes later, James stood on the top of the steps in front of the door. He watched an old Muslim in a keffiyeh pass through the archway without incident. Two of the mujahedeen turned his way, their coal-black eyes drilling holes though his. James waited silently. Finally one of the bearded men nodded.

The former SEAL advanced through the metal detector and walked on, feeling the black eyes still on his back. He entered a court, seeing a tank for ceremonial ablutions, then stepped into the large room ahead. A pulpit and lectern stood at the front of the room, and a niche indicated the direction of Mecca. Unlike a Christian church or Jewish temple, the mosque contained no seats. Instead, carpets covered the concrete floor. Several dozen men knelt, facing the direction in which the niche pointed.

A few of the men looked up as he entered, giving him the same suspicious stare he had gotten on the front steps. James ignored them, taking a place in the center of the room. The thick bandage cut deeper into his ribs as he began to mumble quietly under his breath.

The Phoenix Force warrior knew why he was being scrutinized—his was the only black face present. The other men all wore the medium-brown skin that indicated Arab, rather than African, descent.

His eyes closed, James spoke softly under his breath. While black Muslims were hardly a rarity throughout the world, they appeared to be in this particular mosque. But while it made him stand out to a certain extent, his skin also provided him an excuse not to speak the language should he be approached directly. And if he could put together a legitimate-sounding string of the few Zulu and Swahili words he had picked up over the years, he stood a good chance of passing as an African devotee of Islam.

As he prayed, James's half-closed eyes surveyed the room. Men came and went, disappearing through doorways, then returning. Wherever the secret door was hidden, he felt certain it wasn't in the prayer room, and finally he stood and wandered toward one of the doors through which he'd seen several other men leave.

The Stony Man warrior found himself alone in a long narrow hallway. Where were the terrorists, and where was Sally Coleman? He and the other members of Phoenix Force had learned through another radio call by Goldberg that the rear admiral had been John Buxton Coleman, a strong nominee for vice admiral and a possible fleet commander someday. Sally, his only child, was eighteen years old.

James reached the end of the hall, opened a door and saw that it did indeed lead to a side street outside the mosque. He paused.

His orders from Katz had been to locate the hidden room, then report back. Under no circumstances was he to try to rescue Sally Coleman alone.

Closing the door, the former SEAL turned back toward the prayer room. So far, he didn't have a clue as to where the entrance to the room might be. But he had learned one thing.

The mujahedeen, as well as the other worshipers, were on guard for anything out of the ordinary. What it all boiled down to was that Katz, dark-complected and fluent in Arabic *might* be able to get in. Encizo, with the same coloring, stood a chance of passing, as long as he wasn't required to speak.

But McCarter and Manning? They'd stand out like Calvin James at a Ku Klux Klan convention. The simple fact was that two-fifths of Phoenix Force would be useless on this mission.

James moved slowly back down the hall, coming to a door he'd passed a moment earlier. Taking a deep breath, he cracked it open and peered inside. A kitchen. The lights were off, and though he couldn't see the whole room, no one appeared to be inside.

Footsteps sounded, nearing the hallway. James hesitated, then pushed the kitchen door open and slipped in. He left the door cracked, listening to the voices outside. Arabic. He couldn't understand the language, but the words had a definite conspiratorial tone.

James heard the other door in the hallway open, then the voices disappeared.

The Phoenix Force commando slipped silently back out into the hall, moved to the door and pressed his ear against the wood. He heard the sound of something sliding across the concrete, then the same sound again. He waited for a count of ten, then cracked the door.

Inside, he saw a storage room. Several chairs, bed mats and cooking utensils from the kitchen had been stacked along a side wall. The only other furniture was an empty china cabinet against the far wall. The two men he had heard were nowhere to be seen.

James entered the room quickly and closed the door behind him. He turned toward the china cabinet, his gaze falling to the scraped concrete where it had slid across the floor countless times.

He had no doubt that he had found the entrance to the secret room. But he had a decision to make now.

Should he go back and inform the rest of Phoenix Force, then help plan Sally Coleman's rescue? He had been ordered to, and the Phoenix Force warrior's brain told him to follow that order.

James's heart didn't agree. He had seen the way the eyes in the mosque had followed him until it had appeared he was leaving the building. McCarter and Manning would never pass the scrutiny of those eyes, and even Katz and Encizo were doubtful. To try would risk blowing the whole operation, and might lead to Sally Coleman's death.

The Stony Man warrior made his decision quickly. He would push on, get more Intel, then decide whether to return to the van or attempt the rescue himself. How much farther he went, the ex-SEAL decided, would be determined by what he found.

But as he moved toward the china cabinet, the door behind him suddenly opened.

James whirled, drawing one of the wooden fléchettes from the right pocket of his robe, as one of the bearded mujahedeen stepped into the storage room. The man's eyes held the blaze of the religious fanatic. His hand held a Tokarev 9 mm pistol.

James dived forward, thrusting the fragile wooden instrument at the bearded man's chest. He felt the needle point pierce the robe, the mujahedeen's skin, then stop. He pushed again, driving the weapon into the sternum.

The man looked into James's eyes, startled. The Tokarev fell from his hand, bouncing across the concrete floor.

The wooden knives had been narrowed at the ricasso, and James twisted his wrist violently. The blade snapped off inside the man as he fell to the floor.

The Phoenix Force warrior had bent to retrieve the Tokarev when the second mujahedeen stepped into the room. James drew another wooden weapon, bringing it up in an underhand arch and driving it into the man's throat.

Blood gushed from the puncture as the former SEAL snapped the wood in two again. Another 9 mm pistol, this time a Makarov, dropped to the floor.

James dived for it, but a third guard burst into the room, crashing into the commando as he bent to retrieve the gun. The two men hit the hard concrete together, rolling. The man from Stony Man Farm fought desperately to pull the third and final fléchette from his pocket.

The mujahedeen screamed in rage as he rolled on top of Calvin James and raised a long dagger over his head.

James caught the terrorist's hand as the weapon descended. Drawing the last wooden knife from his robe, he drove it into the man's groin.

The mujahedeen's second scream made the first pale by comparison.

James snapped the grip from the wood, leaving the rest of the weapon buried in the man's scrotum. The former SEAL wrenched the dagger from his attacker's hand, then plunged it into the heart beneath the muslin vest.

The Phoenix Force warrior rolled out from under the corpse and jumped to his feet. There was no chance of going farther now. The screams would bring other men. All he could do at this point was to get the hell out of the mosque and back to the van, where another plan could be formulated.

James stooped, grabbed both pistols, turned toward the door, then stopped dead in his tracks.

Four more mujahedeen stood just outside the door in the hall. All held Uzi submachine guns that were equipped with laser sighting devices.

James looked down at his chest. On top of his robe, just over the heart, four tiny red spots danced on the fabric.

Stony Man Farm

THE WAR ROOM at Stony Man Farm had seemed somber to Mack Bolan when he'd watched it via satellite from Dublin. Now, watching it through the one-way mirror from outside in the hall, the bright lights did nothing to keep it from looking downright dreary.

The lights shone down from the ceiling, reflecting off the bare white walls and mirrored side of the window through which the Executioner watched. The conference table where Hal Brognola, Aaron Kurtzman and Able Team had sat earlier had been removed from the room.

A lone, straight-backed wooden chair now stood in the middle of the room, the only furniture. The man with the handlebar mustache—the Huntsman Bolan had brought back from the Bahamas only a few short hours earlier—sat bound to the chair. During the flight back to Stony Man, the Huntsman had used everything from his own handcuffed hands at his throat to his teeth upon his wrists in vain attempts to kill himself.

The Executioner's eyes moved from the man in the chair to the woman who stood next to him. Dr. Vivian Brookshaus, a longtime friend of Able Team psychological warfare expert Rosario Blancanales, had been flown to the Farm wearing a blindfold. The blindfold hadn't disturbed the woman. As America's top cult deprogrammer, she had worked for the CIA as well as Stony Man many times in the past.

Bolan watched the doctor lean forward and whisper something into the man's ear. Then footsteps on the stairs caused the warrior to turn in time to see Hal Brognola coming down the steps. The Stony Man director wore crumpled gray slacks and an equally wrinkled white shirt and tie. A well-aged Colt Detective Special, the blueing almost nonexistent after years of use, hung from his equally worn belt in a cross-draw holster. A small two-way pager had been clipped onto the big Fed's belt.

The Justice man stopped next to Bolan. "Any change?" he asked.

Bolan nodded. "Slow, but sure. He no longer thinks he's a Huntsman. Now he's some guy named Alexander De Moray."

Brognola pulled a cigar stump from his shirt pocket and shoved it between his teeth. "Aaron know about this yet?"

The warrior shook his head. "It just now came out. I was about to go tell him."

"I'll save you the trip upstairs." The Justice man pulled the pager from his belt and held it to his lips. "Aaron, find out what we know about anybody by the name of Alexander De Moray," he said, then spelled it.

"You run his fingerprints yet?" Bolan asked, nodding toward the window.

Brognola nodded. "Aaron just got them back. His real name's Norman Hlabka. Former Omaha cop. Turns out it was his wife that Lyons talked to earlier. The alcoholic."

More footsteps sounded on the steps, then Barbara Price joined the two men. "Akira just got the skinny back on the security businesses," she said. "There's blinds and dodges like you wouldn't believe. But you dig deep enough, and it turns out every last one of them is owned by the same parent company."

Brognola and Bolan waited.

"Fortress Arms," Price said. "Anybody know a guy named Hayden Thone?"

"The Thone family," Bolan replied, "has manufactured arms for centuries. At one time they were bigger than the Krupps."

Brognola had begun to add something when Dr. Vivian Brookshaus turned and walked toward the door next to the mirror. Bolan hit the code, the door buzzed and a moment later she entered the hall.

"Is there somewhere we can talk?" the woman asked.

Brognola led the way up the steps to the den, ushering Brookshaus into an overstuffed easy chair while he and Bolan took seats across from her. Price retured to her station.

Brookshaus took a deep breath, toying with the eyeglasses that hung around her neck on a chain. "I had heard that experiments of this nature were being conducted, but I had no idea they were this far advanced."

"What are you talking about?" Brognola asked.

"Alters," Brookshaus said bluntly. "Alternate personalities. What you've got here is a man who has been convinced that he's another man."

"Brainwashed?" Brognola asked.

Brookshaus shrugged. "Only a remote resemblance. I'll prepare a detailed report, of course, but let me give you a general idea first. Basically a brand-new personality has been overlaid on top of the old one. Norman Hlabka is still in there, all right, but he's buried so deep he doesn't know it. I think I can get him out, but it'll take time."

Bolan leaned forward in his chair. "So what you're saying, Doctor, is that somebody programmed this man—and other men and women—to act like someone else."

"Not act like," Brookshaus said quickly. "Become. They've actually had this other party's personality entered into their brain."

Brognola bit down on his cigar. "Clones, then?"

"Well, not physical clones. But to call it 'personality cloning' probably wouldn't be too far off."

"But why?" the big Fed asked.

Brookshaus shrugged. "The why isn't my field."

Bolan cleared his throat. "Suppose you had this technology at your disposal, Hal," he said, "and suppose you wanted to create a race of superwarriors for some nefarious plan you had in mind. What would you do?"

Brognola didn't hesitate. "If I wanted superwarriors, and I'm understanding this all correctly, I'd overlay *your* personality on top of as many other people as I could get my hands on."

The warrior shook his head. "It wouldn't work. I don't take or follow orders I don't believe in. You use me as your base, all you'd have is an army that'd tell you to shove it when you ordered them to rob, or steal, or assassinate innocent people."

Brognola nodded. "Okay," he said slowly, thinking. "But if I could find someone with your fighting skills who didn't have your moral standards, say a talented and well-trained mercenary who wouldn't hesitate to sell out to the highest bidder..."

"Then you'd have your man." Bolan turned to Dr. Brookshaus. "Any idea why they went to so much trouble to get such specific people to the casino that night?"

Brookshaus closed her eyes. "As I understand it, they picked former police and military personnel. That would mean these people already had some of the skills necessary. Remember, it's personality we are transplanting, not acquired skills. Shooting, stalking—whatever you people call the things that you do—it's learned behavior and has to be taught."

"But their training was speeded up by using subjects who were well acquainted with the subject already?" Brognola asked.

"It sounds like it to me," Brookshaus said.

"To me, too," Bolan agreed. "What was implanted wasn't the techniques of murder, but a personality that had the emotional ability to commit murder."

Dr. Brookshaus nodded. "A killer without the ability for remorse. No conscience."

"But whose personality did they pick to transplant? Who was the original Huntsman?" Bolan shifted uneasily in his seat. A thought was trying to work its way from his brain to his tongue. It was almost there when Brognola's two-way suddenly beeped.

Brognola pulled the beeper from his belt and pressed a button. "Go ahead, Aaron," he said, then tapped another button turning the device into a speakerphone.

"I've IDed this De Moray," Kurtzman stated. "I'm surprised we haven't run across him before. This guy's a daisy, all right. You're not going to believe him."

There was a moment of silence in the room, then the thought that had fought to surface suddenly materialized in the Executioner's brain. "I believe him," Bolan said. "De Moray's about six feet tall, has black hair, dark skin and eyes that look like tiny chunks of coal."

Kurtzman chuckled over the pager. "Striker, you sure you aren't standing behind me looking at this computer sketch?"

"I don't have to. I saw the real thing in Monaco."

"The man with the potassium," Brognola said. "See if you can track down his whereabouts, Aaron. If he's here in the U.S., I'll send Able—"

Bolan shook his head. "He's mine, Hal."

"I'll send Striker.

Price suddenly stuck her head in the den. "Katz is on the line," she said. "Hal, Striker, maybe you both better come in here."

Bolan and Brognola rose and followed the mission controller into the Communications Room. Price activated her speakerphone, and Yakov Katzenelenbogen's voice came over the airwaves. "Are they there, Barbara?"

"Affirmative, Katz. Go ahead."

"I will give you the details," the former Mossad man stated. "But first, here it is in a nutshell. We have lost Calvin James."

Bolan felt a lump start in his throat. "What do you mean, lost? Is he dead?"

Katz hesitated, then said, "I do not know. But it is possible." He went on to fill in the Stony Man crew on the Bloody Wind kidnapping and James's infiltration of the mosque in Rome.

Bolan listened, then stood as quietly as the rest of the people in the comm room. He wanted Alexander De Moray, but more than that he wanted Calvin James safe.

Without a word, Bolan turned and started for the door.

"Where are you going, Striker?" Brognola asked.

"Rome," the Executioner said simply.

And a moment later, he was gone.

* * * * *

Don't miss the exciting conclusion of The Arms Trilogy. Look for The Executioner #197, Armed Force, *in May.*

**Terrorists are gunning for U.S. blood—and
Mideast powers are picking up the tab**

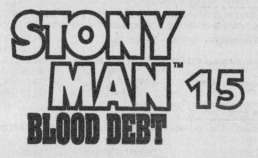

STONY MAN™ 15
BLOOD DEBT

Operating out of mission-control base in Virginia, equipped
with state-of-the-art weapons, surveillance and intelligence-
gathering systems, America's best cybernetics geniuses and
paramilitary commandos wage an endless war of attrition
against the enemies of the free world.

**Don't miss out on the action in these titles featuring
THE EXECUTIONER®, ABLE TEAM® and PHOENIX FORCE®!**

The Terror Trilogy

Features Mack Bolan, along with ABLE TEAM and PHOENIX FORCE, as
they battle neo-Nazis and Arab terrorists to prevent war in the Middle East.

The Executioner #61186	FIRE BURST	$3.50 U.S. $3.99 CAN.	☐ ☐
The Executioner #61187	CLEANSING FLAME	$3.50 U.S. $3.99 CAN.	☐ ☐
SuperBolan #61437	INFERNO	$4.99 U.S. $5.50 CAN.	☐ ☐

The Executioner®

Nonstop action, as Mack Bolan represents ultimate justice, within or beyond
the law.

#61184	DEATH WARRANT	$3.50	☐
#61185	SUDDEN FURY	$3.50	☐
#61188	WAR PAINT	$3.50 U.S. $3.99 CAN.	☐ ☐
#61189	WELLFIRE	$3.50 U.S. $3.99 CAN.	☐ ☐

(limited quantities available on certain titles)

TOTAL AMOUNT	$
POSTAGE & HANDLING	$
($1.00 for one book, 50¢ for each additional)	
APPLICABLE TAXES*	$_____
TOTAL PAYABLE	$_____
(check or money order—please do not send cash)	

To order, complete this form and send it, along with a check or money order for
the total above, payable to Gold Eagle Books, to: **In the U.S.:** 3010 Walden Avenue,
P.O. Box 9077, Buffalo, NY 14269-9077; **In Canada:** P.O. Box 636, Fort Erie, Ontario,
L2A 5X3.

Name:_____

Address:_____ City:_____

State/Prov.:_____ Zip/Postal Code:_____

*New York residents remit applicable sales taxes.
 Canadian residents remit applicable GST and provincial taxes.

GEBACK9